**ERL...
G...**

- Cited by the Guinness Book of World Records as the #1 best-selling writer of all time!

- Author of more than 150 clever, authentic, and sophisticated mystery novels!

- Creator of the amazing Perry Mason, the savvy Della Street, and dynamite detective Paul Drake!

- THE ONLY AUTHOR WHO OUT-SELLS AGATHA CHRISTIE, HAROLD ROBBINS, BARBARA CARTLAND, AND LOUIS L'AMOUR *COMBINED!*

Why?

Because he writes the best, most fascinating whodunits of all!

You'll want to read every one of them, coming soon from
BALLANTINE BOOKS

The Case of the
Gilded Lily

Erle Stanley Gardner

BALLANTINE BOOKS • **NEW YORK**

ISBN 0-345-32318-1

This edition published by arrangement with
William Morrow & Co. Inc.

Manufactured in the United States of America

First Ballantine Books Edition: October 1985

FOREWORD

MY FRIEND DR. WALTER CAMP IS AN OUTSTANDING FIGure in the field of legal medicine.

One of his greatest attributes is the calm detached manner with which he approaches any scientific problem. It is impossible to think of Dr. Camp ever being "stampeded" so that he would lose his intellectual integrity on the one hand, or on the other hand let any personal or financial considerations color his judgment.

Dr. Camp is both an M.D. and a Ph.D., yet despite his intellectual and scientific achievements, and a brain which functions as unemotionally (and as accurately) as an adding machine, he remains a warm, friendly human being.

Dr. Camp is one of the country's leading toxicologists. He is a Professor of Toxicology and Pharmacology at the University of Illinois and is Coroner's Toxicologist for Cook County, which includes the seething metropolis of Chicago.

For the past couple of years he has been Secretary of the American Academy of Forensic Sciences, and heaven knows how much time, energy and time-consuming effort he and his personal secretary, Polly Cline, have poured into that organization.

Dr. Camp is no prima donna with a temperament, although his achievements and record would entitle him to develop all the idiosyncrasies of temperament; on the contrary, he loves to work with others, to become a member of a "team," and then to minimize his own part in that team's achievement.

Such men, who have the ability to get things done, who have the executive qualities necessary to co-ordinate the work of others, and the stability necessary to work with others, are rare.

This year, the annual meeting of the Academy of Forensic Sciences was held under the guidance of Dr. Camp, Secretary; Fred Inbau (Professor of Criminal Law at Northwestern University), President; and Dr. Richard Ford (head of the Department of Legal Medicine at Harvard University), Program Chairman. Those of us who attended found it one of the most inspirational and informative academy sessions ever to be held in an organization covering such a complex field. This was due mainly to the fact that these three men worked together as a team with such perfect co-ordination, such smooth co-operation, and such clockwork efficiency that many of us failed to realize the untold hours of planning, working, and almost constant consultation which made the extraordinary results possible.

Dr. Camp has worked on many a spectacular case where anyone less cool, less objective in his approach, would have been swept off his scientific feet. There was for instance the famous Ragen case where a man on the receiving end of a shotgun blast was later claimed to have died because of mercuric poisoning. There was another famous case: that of a gangster awaiting execution in the electric chair who beat the executioner to the punch, reportedly with the aid of a lethal dose of strychnine.

Dr. Camp, as a referee in these cases, handled himself in a manner which was a credit to the best traditions of forensic science. He refused to be influenced by rumors, the pressures of interested parties, or popular excitement. He approached the problems as a scientist, and he solved them as a scientist.

And so I dedicate this book to my friend:

WALTER J. R. CAMP, M.D., PH.D.

—Erle Stanley Gardner

CAST OF CHARACTERS

■ 1 ■

STEWART G. BEDFORD ENTERED HIS PRIVATE OFFICE, hung up his hat, walked across to the huge walnut desk which had been a birthday present from his wife a year ago, and eased himself into the swivel chair.

His secretary, Elsa Griffin, with her never failing and characteristic efficiency, had left the morning paper on his desk, the pages neatly folded back so that Mrs. Bedford's photograph was smiling up at him from the printed page.

It was a good picture of Ann Roann Bedford, bringing out the little characteristic twinkle in her eyes, the sparkle and vitality of her personality.

Stewart Bedford was very, very proud of his wife. Mixed with that pride was the thrill of possession, the feeling that he, at fifty-two, had been able to marry a woman twenty years his junior and make her radiantly happy.

Bedford, with his wealth, his business contacts, his influential friends, had never paid attention to social life. His first wife had been dead for some twelve years. After her death the social circle of their friends would have liked to consider Stewart G. Bedford as the "most eligible bachelor," but Bedford wanted no part of it. He immersed himself in his business, continued to enhance his financial success, and took almost as much pride in the growing influence of his name in the business world as he would have taken in a son if he had had one.

Then he had met Ann Roann and his life suddenly slipped into a tailspin that caused a whirlwind courtship to culminate in a Nevada marriage.

Ann was as pleased with the social position she acquired through her marriage as a child with a new toy. Bedford still maintained his interest in his business, but it was no longer the dominant factor in his life. He wanted to get Ann Roann the things out of life which would make her happy, and Ann Roann had a long list of such things. However, her quick, enthusiastic response, her obvious gratitude, left Bedford constantly feeling like an indulgent parent on Christmas morning.

Bedford had settled himself at his desk and was reading the paper when Elsa Griffin glided in.

"Good morning, Elsa," he said. "Thanks for calling my attention to the account of Mrs. Bedford's party."

Her smile acknowledged his thanks. It was a nice smile.

To Stewart, Elsa Griffin was as comfortable as a smoking jacket and slippers. She had been with him for fifteen years; she knew his every want, his every whim, and had an uncanny ability to read his mind. He was very, very fond of her; in fact, there had been a romantic interlude after his first wife died. Elsa's quiet understanding had been one of the great things in his life. He had even considered marrying her—but that was before he had met Ann Roann.

Bedford knew he had made a fool of himself falling head over heels in love with Ann Roann, a woman who was just entering her thirties. He knew the hurt he was inflicting on Elsa Griffin, but he could no more control his actions than water rushing down a stream could stop on the brink of a precipice. He had plunged on into matrimony.

Elsa Griffin had offered her congratulations and wishes for every happiness and had promptly faded back into the position of the trusted private secretary. If she had suffered—and he was sure she had—there was no sign visible to the naked eye.

"There's a man waiting to see you," Elsa Griffin said.

"Who is he? What does he want?"

"His name is Denham. He said to tell you that Binney Denham wanted to see you and would wait."

"Benny Denham?" Bedford said. "I don't know any Benny Denham. How does it happen he wants to see me? Let him see one of the executives who—"

"It's not Benny. It's Binney," she said, "and he says it's a personal matter, that he'll wait until he can see you."

Bedford made a gesture of dismissal with his hand.

Elsa shook her head. "I don't think he'll leave. He really intends to see you."

Bedford scowled. "I can't be accessible to every Tom, Dick and Harry that comes in and says he wants to see me on a personal matter."

"I know," she said, "but Mr. Denham ... there's something about him that's just a little ... it's hard to describe ... a persistence that's ... well, it's a little frightening."

"Frightening!" Bedford said, bristling.

"Not in that way. It's just the fact that he has this terrible, deadly patience. You get the feeling that it would really be better to see him. He sits in the chair, quiet and motionless, and ... and every time I look up he's looking at me with those peculiar eyes. I do wish you'd see him, S. G. I have a feeling you should."

"All right," Bedford said. "What the hell! Let's see what he wants and get rid of him. A personal matter. Not an old school friend that wants a touch?"

"No, no! Nothing like that. Something that ... well, I have the feeling that it's important."

"All right," Bedford said, smiling. "I can always trust your intuition. We'll get him out of the way before we tackle the mail. Send him in."

Elsa left the office, and a few moments later Binney Denham was standing in the doorway bowing and smiling apologetically. Only his eyes were not apologetic. They were steady and appraising, as though his mission were a matter of life and death.

"I'm so glad you'll see me, Mr. Bedford," he said. "I was afraid perhaps I might have trouble. Delbert told me I *had* to see *you,* that I had to wait until I saw you, no matter how long it took, and Delbert is a hard man to cross."

Some inner bell rang a warning in Bedford's mind. He said, "Sit down. And who the devil is Delbert?"

"He's a sort of associate of mine."

"A partner?"

"No, no. I'm not a partner. I'm an associate."

"All right. Sit down. Tell me what it is you want. But you'll have to make it brief. I have some appointments this morning and there's some important mail here which has to be handled."

"Yes, sir. Thank you very much, sir."

Binney Denham moved over and sat on the extreme edge of the chair at the side of the desk. His hat was clutched over his stomach. He hadn't offered to shake hands.

"Well, what is it?" Bedford asked.

"It's about a business investment," Denham said. "It seems that Delbert needs money for financing this venture of his. It will only take twenty thousand dollars and he should be able to pay back the money within a few—"

"Say, what the devil *is* this?" Bedford said. "You told my secretary you wanted to see me about a personal matter. I don't know you. I don't know Delbert, and I'm not interested in financing any business venture to the tune of twenty thousand dollars. Now if that's all you—"

"Oh, but you don't understand, sir," the little man protested. "You see, it involves your wife."

Bedford stiffened with silent anger, but that inner bell which had sounded the note of warning before now gave such a strident signal that he became very cautious.

"And what about my wife?" he asked.

"Well, you see, sir, it's like this. Of course, you understand there's a market for these things now. These maga-

4

zines . . . I'm sure you don't like them any better than I do. I won't even read the things, and I'm quite certain you don't, sir. But you must know of their existence, and they're *very popular*."

"All right," Bedford said. "Get it out of your system. What are you talking about?"

"Well, of course, it . . . well, you almost have to know Delbert, Mr. Bedford, in order to understand the situation. Delbert is very insistent. When he wants something, he *really* wants it."

"All right, go on," Bedford snapped. "What about my wife? Why are you bringing her name into this?"

"Well, of course, I was only mentioning it because . . . well, you see, *I* know Delbert, and, while I don't condone his ideas, I—"

"What are his ideas?"

"He needs money."

"All right, he needs money. So what?"

"He thought you could furnish it."

"And my wife?" Bedford asked, restraining an impulse to throw the little man bodily out of the office.

"Well, of course your wife's record," Denham said.

"What do you mean, her record?"

"Her criminal record, fingerprints, et cetera," Denham said in that same quietly apologetic manner.

There was a moment of frozen silence. Bedford, too accustomed to playing poker in business to let Denham see the slightest flicker of expression on his face, was rapidly thinking back. After all, what did he know about Ann Roann? She had been the victim of an unhappy marriage she didn't like to discuss. There had been some sort of tragedy. Her husband's suicide had been his final confession of futility. There had been some insurance which had enabled the young widow to carry on during a period of readjustment. There had been two years of foreign travel and then she had met Stewart Bedford.

Bedford's own voice sounded strange to him. "Put your cards on the table. What is this? Blackmail?"

"*Blackmail!*" the man exclaimed with every evidence of horror. "Oh, my heavens, no, Mr. Bedford! Good heavens, no! Even Delbert wouldn't stoop to anything like that."

"Well, what *is* it?" Bedford asked.

"I'd like an opportunity to explain about the business investment. I think you'll agree it's a very sound investment and you could have the twenty thousand back within . . . well, Delbert says six months. I personally think it would be more like a year. Delbert's always optimistic."

"What about my wife's record?" Bedford's voice now definitely had a rasp to it.

"Well, of course, that's the point," Denham said apologetically. "You see, sir, Delbert simply *has* to have the money, and he thought you might loan it to him. Then, of course, he has this information and he knows that some of these magazines pay very high prices for tips. I've talked it over with him. I feel certain that they wouldn't pay anything like twenty thousand, but Delbert thinks they would if the information was fully authenticated and—"

"This information is authenticated?" Bedford asked.

"Oh, of course, sir, of course! I wouldn't even have mentioned it otherwise."

"How is it authenticated?"

"What the police call mug shots and fingerprints."

"Let me see."

"I'd much prefer to talk about the investment, Mr. Bedford. I didn't really intend to bring it up in this way. However, I could see you were rather impatient about—"

"What about the information?" Bedford asked.

The little man let go of the rim of his hat with his right hand. He fished in an inner pocket and brought out a plain Manila envelope.

"I'm sure I hadn't intended to tell you about it in this way," he said sorrowfully.

He extended the Manila envelope toward Bedford.

Bedford took the envelope, turned back the flap, and pulled out the papers that were on the inside.

It was either the damnedest clever job of fake photography he had ever seen or it was Ann Roann . . . Ann Roann's picture taken some years earlier. There was the same daring, don't-give-a-damn sparkle in her eyes, the lilt to her head, the twist of her lips, and down underneath was that damning serial number, below that a set of fingerprints and the sections of the penal code that had been violated.

Denham's voice droned on, filling in the gap in Bedford's thinking.

"Those sections of the penal code relate to insurance fraud, if you don't mind, Mr. Bedford. I know you're curious. I was too when I looked it up."

"What's she supposed to have done?" Bedford asked.

"She had some jewelry that was insured. She made the mistake of pawning the jewelry before she reported that it had been stolen. She collected on the insurance policy, and then they found where the jewelry had been pawned and . . . well, the police are very efficient in such matters."

"What was done with the charge?" Bedford asked. "Was she convicted, given probation? Was the charge dismissed, or what?"

"Heavens! *I* don't know," Denham said. "I'm not sure that even Delbert knows. These are the records that Delbert gave me. He said that he was going to take them to this magazine and that they'd pay him for the tip. I told him I thought he was being very, very foolish, that I didn't think the magazine would pay as much as he needed for his investment, and frankly, Mr. Bedford, I don't like such things. I don't like those magazines or this business of assassinating character, of digging up things out of a person's dead past. I just don't like it."

"I see," Bedford said grimly. He sat there holding in

front of him the photostatic copy of the circular describing his wife—age, height, weight, eye color, fingerprint classification.

So this was blackmail. He'd heard about it. Now he was up against it. This little man sitting there on the edge of the chair, holding his hat across his stomach, his hands clutching the rim, his manner apologetic, was a blackmailer and Bedford was being given the works.

Bedford knew all about what he was supposed to do under such circumstances. He was supposed to throw the little bastard out of his office, beat him up, turn him over to the police. He was supposed to tell him, "Go ahead. Do your damnedest! I won't pay a dime for blackmail!" Or he was supposed to string the man along, ring up the police department, explain the matter to the officer in charge of such things, a man who would promise to handle it discreetly and keep it very, very confidential.

He knew how such things were handled. They would arrange for him to turn over marked money. Then they would arrest Binney Denham and the case would be kept very hush-hush.

But would it?

There was this mysterious Delbert in the background . . . Delbert, who apparently was the ringleader of the whole thing . . . Delbert, who wanted to sell his information to one of those magazines that were springing up like mushrooms, magazines which depended for their living on exploiting sensational facts about people in the public eye.

Either these were police records or they weren't.

If they were police records, Bedford was trapped. There was no escape. If they weren't police records, it was a matter of forgery.

"I'd want some time to look into this," he said.

"How much time?" Binney Denham asked, and for the first time there was a certain hard note in his voice that caused Bedford to look up sharply, but his eyes saw only a little man sitting timidly on the very edge of the chair, holding his hat on his stomach.

"Well, for one thing, I'd want to verify the facts."

"Oh, you mean in the business deal?" Denham asked, his voice quick with hope.

"The business deal be damned!" Bedford said. "You know what this is and I know what it is. Now get the hell out of here and let me think."

"Oh, but I wanted to tell you about the business deal," Denham said. "Delbert is certain you'll have every penny of your money back. It's just a question of raising some operating capital, Mr. Bedford, and—"

"I know. I know," Bedford interrupted. "Give me time to think this over."

Binney Denham got to his feet at once. "I'm sorry I intruded on you without an appointment, Mr. Bedford. I know how busy you are. I realize I must have taken up a lot of your time. I'll go now."

"Wait a minute," Bedford said. "How do I get in touch with you?"

Binney Denham turned in the doorway. "Oh, *I'll* get in touch with *you,* sir, if you don't mind, sir. And of course I'll have to talk with Delbert. Good day, sir!" and the little man opened the door a crack and slipped away.

■ 2 ■

Dinner that night was a tete-a-tete affair with Ann Roann Bedford serving the cocktails herself on a silver tray which had been one of the wedding presents.

Stewart Bedford felt thoroughly despicable as he slid

the tray face down under the davenport while Ann Roann was momentarily in the serving pantry.

Later on, after a dinner during which he tried in vain to conceal the tension he was laboring under, he got the tray up to his study, attached it to a board with adhesive tape around the edges so that any latent fingerprints on the bottom would not be disfigured, and then fitted it in a pasteboard box in which he had recently received some shirts.

Ann Roann commented on the box the next day when her husband left for work carrying it under his arm. He told her in what he hoped was a casual manner that the color of the shirts hadn't been satisfactory and he was going to exchange them. He said he'd get Elsa Griffin to wrap and mail the package.

For a moment Bedford thought that there was a fleeting mistrust in his wife's slate gray eyes, but she said nothing and her good-by kiss was a clinging pledge of the happiness that had come to mean so much to him.

Safely ensconced in his private office, Bedford went to work on a problem that he knew absolutely nothing about. He had stopped at the art store downstairs to buy some drawing charcoal and a camel's-hair brush. He rubbed the edge of the stick of drawing charcoal into fine dust and dusted this over the bottom of the tray. He was pleased to find that he had developed several perfectly legible latent fingerprints.

It now remained to compare those fingerprints with the fingerprints on the criminal record which had been left him by the apologetic little man who needed the "loan" of twenty thousand dollars.

So engrossed was Stewart Bedford in what he was doing that he didn't hear Elsa Griffin enter the office.

She was standing by his side at the desk, looking over his shoulder, before he glanced up with a start.

"I didn't want to be disturbed," he said irritably.

"I know," she said in that voice of quiet understanding. "I thought perhaps I could be of help."

"Well, you can't."

She said, "The technique used by detectives is to take a piece of transparent cellophane tape and place it over the latent fingerprints. Then when you remove the Scotch tape the dust adheres to the tape and you can put the print on a card and study it at leisure without damaging the latent print."

Stewart Bedford whirled around in his chair. "Look here," he said. "Just how much do you know and what are you talking about?"

She said, "Perhaps you didn't remember, but you left the intercommunicating system open to my desk when you were talking with Mr. Denham yesterday."

"The devil I did!"

She nodded.

"I wasn't conscious of it. I'm almost sure I shut it off."

She shook her head. "You didn't."

"All right," he said. "Go get me some cellophane tape. We'll try it."

"I have some here," she said. "Also a pair of scissors."

Her long, skillful fingers deftly snipped pieces of the transparent tape, laid them over the back of the silver tray, smoothed them into position, and then removed the tape so they could study the fingerprints, line for line, whorl for whorl.

"You seem to know something about this," Bedford said.

She laughed. "Believe it or not, I once took a correspondence course in how to be a detective."

"Why?"

"I'm darned if I know," she admitted cheerfully. "I just wanted something to do and I've always been fascinated with problems of detection. I thought it might sharpen my powers of observation."

Bedford patted her affectionately. "Well, if you're so

darn good at it, draw up a chair and sit down. Take this magnifying glass and let's see what we can find out."

Elsa Griffin had, as it turned out, a considerable talent for matching fingerprints. She knew what to look for and how to find the different points of similarity. In a matter of fifteen minutes Stewart Bedford came to the sickening realization that there could be no doubt about it. The fingerprints on the police record were an identical match for the four perfect latents which had been lifted from the silver tray.

"Well," Bedford said, "since you know all about it, what suggestions do you have, Elsa?"

She shook her head. "This is a problem you have to solve for yourself, S. G. If you once start paying, there's no end to it."

"And if I don't?" he asked.

She shrugged her shoulders.

Bedford looked down at the silver tray which reflected a distorted image of his own harassed features. He knew what it would mean to Ann Roann to have something of this sort come out.

She was so full of life, vivacity, happiness. Bedford could visualize what would happen if one of these magazines that were becoming so popular should come out with the story of Ann Roann's past; the story of an adventurous girl who had sought to finance her venture into the matrimonial market by defrauding an insurance company.

No matter what the alternative, he couldn't let that happen.

There would, he knew, be frigid expressions of sympathy, the formal denunciation of "those horrible scandal sheets." There would be an attempt on the part of some to be "charitable" to Ann Roann. Others would cut her at once, deliberately and coldly.

Gradually the circle would tighten. Ann Roann would have to plead a nervous breakdown . . . a foreign cruise somewhere. She would never come back—not the way Ann Roann would want to come back.

Elsa Griffin seemed to be reading his mind.

"You might," she said, "play along with him for a while; stall for time as much as possible, but try to find out something about who this man is. After all, he must have his own weaknesses.

"I remember reading a story one time where a man was faced with a somewhat similar problem and—"

"Yes?" Bedford said as she paused.

"Of course, it was just a story."

"Go ahead."

"The man couldn't afford to deny their blackmail claims. He didn't dare to have the thing they were holding over him become public, but he . . . well, he was clever and . . . of course, it was just a story. There were two of them just as there are here."

"Go on! What did he do?"

"He killed one of the blackmailers and made the evidence indicate the other blackmailer had committed the murder. The frantic blackmailer tried to tell the true story to the jury, but the jury just laughed at him and sent him to the electric chair."

"That's farfetched," Bedford said. "It could only work in a story."

"I know," she said. "It was just a story, but it was so convincingly told that it . . . well, it just seemed terribly plausible. I remembered it. It stuck in my mind."

Bedford looked at her in amazement, seeing a new phase of her character which he had never dreamed existed.

"I never knew you were so bloodthirsty, Elsa."

"It was only a story."

"But you stored it in your mind. How did you become interested in this detective business?"

"Through reading the magazines which feature true crime stories."

"You like them?"

"I love them."

Again he looked at her.

"They keep your mind busy," she explained.

"I guess I'm learning a lot about people very fast," he said, still studying her.

"A girl has to have *something* to occupy her mind when she's left all alone," she said defensively but not defiantly.

He hastily looked back at the tray, then gently put it back in the shirt box. "We'll just have to wait it out now, Elsa. Whenever Denham calls on the telephone or tries to get in touch with me, stall him off if you can. But when he gets insistent, put the call through. I'll talk with him."

"What about these?" she asked, indicating the lifted fingerprints on the Scotch tape.

"Destroy them," Bedford said. "Get rid of them. And don't just put them in a wastebasket. Cut them into small pieces with scissors and burn them."

She nodded and quietly left the office.

There was no word from Binney Denham all that day. It got so his very failure to try to communicate got on Bedford's nerves. Twice during the afternoon he called Elsa in.

"Anything from Denham?"

She shook her head.

"Never mind trying to stall him," Bedford said. "When he calls, put the call through. If he comes to see me, let him come in. I can't stand the strain of this suspense. Let's find out what we're up against as soon as we can."

"Do you want a firm of private detectives?" she asked. "Would you like to have them shadow him when he leaves the office and—"

"Hell, no!" Bedford said. "How do I know that I could trust the private detectives? They might shadow him and find out all about what he knows. Then I'd be paying blackmail to two people instead of one. Let's keep this on a basis where we're handling it ourselves . . . and, of course, there *is* a possibility that the guy is right. It may be just a loan. It may be that this partner—this Delbert he refers to—is really a screwball who needs some capital and is taking this way of raising it. He may really be hesitating between selling his information to a magazine and letting me advance the loan. Elsa, if Denham telephones, put through the call immediately. I want to get these fellows tied up before there's any possibility they'll peddle that stuff to a magazine. It would be dynamite!"

"All right," she promised. "I'll put him through the minute he calls."

But Binney Denham didn't call, and Bedford went home that evening feeling like a condemned criminal whose application for a commutation of sentence is in the hands of the governor. Every minute became sixty seconds of agonizing suspense.

Ann Roann was wearing a hostess gown which plunged daringly to a low *V* in front and was fastened with an embroidered frog. She had been to the beauty parlor, and her hair glinted with soft high lights.

Stewart Bedford found himself hoping that they would have another tête-à-tête dinner, with candlelight and cocktails, but she reminded him that a few friends were coming in and that he had to change to a dinner coat and black tie.

Bedford lugged the cardboard box up to his room, opened it, tore off the strips of adhesive tape which held the silver cocktail tray to the board, and managed to get the tray down to the serving pantry without being noticed.

The little dinner was a distinct success. Ann Roann was at her best, and Bedford noted with satisfaction the glances that came his way from men who had for years taken him for granted. Now they were looking at him as though appraising some new hidden quality which they had overlooked. There was a combination of envy and admiration in their expressions that made him feel a lot younger than his years. He found himself squaring his shoulders, bringing in his stomach, holding his head erect.

After all, it was a pretty good world. Nothing was so bad that it couldn't be cured somehow. Things were never as bad as they seemed.

Then came the call to the telephone. The butler said that a Mr. D. said the call was quite important, and he was certain that Mr. Bedford would want to be advised.

Bedford made a great show of firmness. "Tell him that I'm not receiving any calls at the moment," he said. "Tell him he can call me at the office tomorrow, or leave me a number where I can call him back in an hour or two."

The butler nodded and vanished, and for a moment Bedford felt as though he had won a point. After all, he'd show these damn blackmailers that he wasn't going to jump every time they snapped their fingers. Then the butler was back.

"Beg your pardon, sir," he said, "but Mr. D. said the message is *most* important, that I was to tell you his associate is getting entirely out of control. He said he'd call you back in twenty minutes, that that was the best he could do."

"Very well," Bedford said, trying to keep up the external semblance of poise, but filled with sudden panic. "I'll talk with him when he calls."

He didn't realize how frequently he was consulting his wrist watch during the next interminable quarter of an hour, until he saw Ann Roann watching him speculatively; then he cursed himself for letting his tension show. He should have gone to the telephone immediately.

None of the guests seemed to notice anything unusual. Only Ann Roann's deep slate eyes followed him with that peculiarly withdrawn look which she had at times when she was thinking something out.

It was exactly twenty minutes from the time of the first call that the butler came to the door. He caught Bedford's

16

eye and nodded. This time Bedford, moving in a manner which he tried to make elaborately casual, started toward the door, said, "All right, Harvey. I'll take the call in my upstairs office. Hang up the downstairs phone as soon as I get on the line."

"Very good, sir," the butler said.

Bedford excused himself to his guests, climbed the stairs hurriedly to his den, closed the door tightly, picked up the receiver, said, "Yes, hello. This is Bedford speaking." He heard Denham's voice filled with apologies.

"I'm terribly sorry I had to disturb you tonight, sir, but I thought you'd like to know. You see, Delbert talked with someone who knows the people who run this magazine and it seems he wouldn't have any difficulty at all getting—"

"Whom did he talk with?" Bedford asked.

"I don't know, sir. I'm sure I don't know. It was just someone who knew about the magazine. It seems that they do pay a lot of money for some of the things they publish and—"

"Bosh and nonsense!" Bedford interrupted. "No scandal sheet is going to pay that sort of money for a tip of that sort. Besides, if they publish I'll sue them for libel."

"Yes, sir. I know. I wish you could talk with Delbert. I think you could convince him. But the point is *I* couldn't convince him. He's going to go to the magazine first thing in the morning. I daresay that when they learn what he has, they'll offer him a very paltry sum, but I thought you'd like to know, sir."

"Now look," Bedford said. "Let's be sensible about this thing. Delbert doesn't want to deal with that magazine. You tell Delbert to get in touch with *me*."

"Oh, Delbert wouldn't do *that*, sir! He's terribly afraid of you, sir."

"Afraid of me?"

"Yes, of course, sir. That's why I . . . well, I thought you'd understand. *I* thought we should tell *you*. I thought we owed you that much out of respect for your position. It was all *my* idea coming to you. Delbert, you see, just wanted to make an outright sale. He says there're certain disadvantages doing business this way, that you might trap him in something. He's . . . well, he doesn't want to do it this way at all. He wants to give the magazine a piece of legitimate news and take whatever they give him as legitimate compensation. He tried to keep me from going to you. He says there's every possibility you could trap us in some way."

"Now look," Bedford said. "This man Delbert is a fool. I am not going to be told what to do and what not to do."

"Yes, sir."

"I'm not going to be terrified by anybody."

"Yes, sir."

"I also know this information is phony. I know there's something cockeyed about it somewhere."

"Oh, I'm sorry to hear you say that, sir, because Delbert—"

"Now, wait a minute," Bedford interrupted. "Just hold your horses. I've told you where *I* stand, but I've also made up my mind that rather than have any trouble about it, I'm willing to go ahead and do what you people want. Now is that clear?"

"Oh, yes, sir. That's very clear! If I can tell Delbert that, it will make him feel *very* much different—that is, I hope it does. Of course, he's afraid that you're too smart for us. He's afraid that you'll lay a trap."

"Trap, nothing!" Bedford said. "Now, let's get this straight. When I do business, I do business on a basis of good faith. My word is good. I'm not setting any traps. Now, you tell Delbert to keep in line, and you call at my office tomorrow and we'll arrange to fix things up."

"I'm afraid it has to be done tonight, sir."

"Tonight! That's impossible!"

"Well, that's all right then," Denham said. "If you feel that way, that's—"

"Wait a minute! Wait a minute!" Bedford shouted. "Don't hang up. I'm just telling you it's impossible to get things lined up for tonight."

"Well, I don't know whether I can hold Delbert in line or not."

"I'll give you a check," Bedford said.

"Oh, good heavens, no, sir! Not a check! Delbert wouldn't ever hear of that, sir. He'd feel certain that was an attempt to trap him. The money would have to be in cash, if you know what I mean, sir. It would have to be money . . . well . . . money that couldn't be traced. Delbert is very suspicious, Mr. Bedford, and he thinks you're a very smart businessman."

"Let's quit playing cops and robbers," Bedford said. "Let's get down to a business basis on this thing. I'll go to the bank tomorrow morning and get some money, and you can—"

"Just a moment, please," Denham's voice said. "Delbert said never mind. Just let the matter drop."

"Let's quit playing cops and robbers," Bedford said. Bedford could hear voices at the other end of the line. He could hear the sound of Denham's pleading, and once or twice he fancied he could hear a gruff voice, then Denham would cut in in that same apologetic drone. He couldn't hear the words, just the tone of voice.

Then Denham was back on the phone again.

"I'll tell you what you do, Mr. Bedford. This is probably the best way of handling it. Now, tomorrow morning just as soon as your bank opens you go to your bank and get twenty thousand dollars in traveler's checks. The checks are to be one hundred dollars each. You get those checks and go to your office and then I'll get in touch with you at your office. I'm awfully sorry I bothered you tonight, Mr. Bedford. I knew we shouldn't have done it. I told Delbert that it was an imposition. But Delbert gets terribly impatient and he *is* suspicious. You see, this deal means a lot to him, and . . . well, you'd have to know him to understand.

"I'm just trying to do the best I can, Mr. Bedford, and it puts *me* in a terribly embarrassing position. I'm terribly sorry I called you."

"Not at all," Bedford heard himself saying. "Now you look here, Denham. You keep this Delbert person, whoever he is, in line. I'll see that you get the money tomorrow. Now don't let him get out of line. You stay with him."

"Yes, sir."

"Can you be with him all the time tonight? Don't let him out of your sight. I don't want him to get any foolish ideas."

"Well, I'll try."

"All right. You do that," Bedford said. "I'll see you tomorrow. Good-by."

He heard Binney Denham hang up, and reached for his handkerchief to wipe the cold sweat on his forehead before dropping the receiver into place. It was then he heard the second unmistakable click on the line.

In an agony of apprehension he tried to remember if he had heard the sound of the butler hanging up the receiver on the lower phone after he came on the line. He had no recollection of the sound.

Was it possible the lower phone had been open during the conversation? Had someone been listening?

Who?

How long had they had this damned butler anyway? Ann Roann had hired him. What did she know about him? Was it possible this whole thing was an inside job?

Who was this damned Delbert? How the devil did he know that there actually was any Delbert at all? How did he know that he wasn't dealing with Denham, and with Denham alone?

Filled with a savage determination, Bedford opened the drawer of his dresser, took out the snub-nosed blued

20

steel .38 caliber gun and shoved it in his brief case. Damn it, if these blackmailers wanted to play tough, he'd be just as tough as they were.

He opened the door from the den, descended the stairs quietly, and then at the foot of the stairs came to a sudden pause as he saw Ann Roann in the butler's pantry. She had found the silver serving tray and was holding it so that the light shone on the back.

The silver tray hadn't been washed and there remained a very faint impression of charcoal-dusted fingerprints, of places where the strips of adhesive tape had left marks on the polished silver.

■ 3 ■

STEWART G. BEDFORD FELT UNREASONABLY ANGRY AS HE signed his name two hundred times to twenty thousand dollars' worth of checks.

The banker, who had tried to make conversation, didn't help matters any.

"Pleasure or business trip, Mr. Bedford?"

"Neither."

"No?"

"No."

Bedford signed his name in savage silence; then, realizing that his manner had only served to arouse curiosity, added, "I like to have some cash reserves on hand these days, something you can convert to cash in a minute."

"Oh, I see," the banker said, and thereafter said nothing.

Bedford folded the checks and left the bank. Why the

devil couldn't they have taken the money in tens and twenties the way they did with kidnap ransom in the movies. Served him right for getting mixed up with a damn bunch of blackmailers.

Bedford entered his private office and found Elsa Griffin sitting there waiting for him.

Bedford raised his eyebrows.

"Mr. Denham and a girl are waiting for you," she said.

"A girl?"

She nodded.

"What sort of a girl?"

"A babe."

"A moll?"

"It's hard to tell. She's really something for looks."

"Describe her."

"Blonde, nice complexion, beautiful legs, plenty of curves, big limpid eyes, a dumb look, a little perfume, and that's all."

"You mean that's really all?"

"That's all there is."

"Well, let's have them in," Bedford said, "and I'll leave the intercom on so you can listen."

"Do you want me to . . . to do anything?"

He shook his head. "There's nothing we can do except give them the money."

Elsa Griffin went out and Binney Denham came in with the blonde.

"Good morning, Mr. Bedford, good morning. I want to introduce you to Geraldine Corning."

The blonde batted her big eyes at him and said in a throaty, seductive voice, "Gerry, for short."

"Now it's like this," Binney Denham said. "You're going out with Gerry."

"What do you mean, going out with her?"

"Going out with me," Gerry said.

"Now look here," Bedford began angrily. "I'm willing to—"

He was stopped by the peculiar look in Binney Denham's eyes.

"This is the way Delbert says it has to be," Denham said. "He has it all figured out, Mr. Bedford. I've been having a lot of trouble with Delbert . . . a whole lot of trouble. I don't think I could explain things to him if there were to be any variation."

"All right," Bedford said angrily. "Let's get it over with."

"You have the checks?"

"I have the checks here in my brief case."

"Well, that's fine! That's just dandy! I told Delbert I knew we could count on you. But he's frightened, and when a man gets frightened he does unreasonable things. Don't you think so, Mr. Bedford?"

"I wouldn't know," Bedford said grimly.

"That's right. You wouldn't, would you?" Binney said. "I'm sorry I asked you the question in that way, Mr. Bedford. I was talking about Delbert. He's a peculiar mixture, and you can say that again."

Gerry's eyes smiled at Bedford. "I think we'd better start."

"Where are we going?" Bedford asked.

"Gerry will tell you. I'll ride down in the elevator with you if you don't mind, Mr. Bedford, and then I'll leave you two. I'm quite certain it will be all right."

Bedford hesitated.

"Of course," Denham said, "I'm terribly sorry it had to work out in this way. I know that you've been inconvenienced enough as it is, and I just want you to know that I've been against it all along, Mr. Bedford. I know that your word is good, and I'd like to deal with you on that basis, but you just can't understand Delbert unless you've had dealings with him. Delbert is terribly suspicious. You see, he's afraid. He feels that you're a smart businessman and that you may have been in touch with somebody who would make trouble. Delbert just wants to

23

go right ahead and make a sale to the magazine. He says that that's perfectly legitimate and no one can——"

"Oh, for heaven's sake!" Bedford exploded. "Let's cut out this comedy. I'm going to pay. I've got the money. You want the money. Now let's go!"

Gerry moved close to him, linked her arm through his, holding it familiarly.

"You heard what he said, Binney. He wants to go."

Bedford made for the door that led to the outer office.

"Not that way," Binney said apologetically. "We're supposed to go out through the exit door directly to the elevator."

"I have to let my secretary know I'm going out," Bedford said, making a last stand. "She *has* to know I'm going out."

Binney coughed. "I'm sorry, sir. Delbert was most insistent on that point."

"Now look here——" Bedford began, then stopped.

"It's better this way, Mr. Bedford. This is the way Delbert wanted it."

Bedford permitted Geraldine Corning to lead him toward the door. Binney Denham held it open and the three of them went out in the corridor, took the express elevator to the ground floor.

"This way," Binney said and escorted them to a new-looking, yellow car which was parked at the curb directly in front of the building.

"Are you worried about women drivers?" Geraldine asked him.

"How good are you?" Bedford asked.

"At driving?"

"Yes."

"Not too good."

"I'll drive."

"Okay by me."

"How about Denham?"

"Oh, Binney's not coming. Binney's all finished. He'll follow for a ways, that's all."

Bedford got in behind the wheel.

The blonde slid gracefully in beside him. She was, Bedford conceded to himself, quite a package—curves in the right places; eyes, complexion, legs, clothes—and yet he couldn't be sure whether she was stupid or putting on an act.

"Bye, Binney," she said.

The little man bowed and smiled and bowed and smiled again. "Have a nice trip," he said as Bedford gunned the engine into life.

"Which way?" he asked.

"Straight ahead," the blonde said.

For one swift moment Bedford had a glimpse of Elsa Griffin on the sidewalk. Thanks to the intercom she had learned their plans in time to get to the sidewalk before they had left the office.

He saw that she was holding a pencil and notebook, He knew she had the license number of the car he was driving.

He managed to keep from looking directly at Elsa and eased the car out into traffic.

"Now, look," Bedford said. "I want to know something about what I'm getting into."

"You aren't afraid of me, are you?"

"I want to know what I'm getting into."

"You do as you're told," she instructed him, "and there won't be any trouble."

"I don't do business that way."

"Then drive back to your office," she said, "and forget the whole business."

Bedford thought that over, then kept driving straight ahead.

The blonde squirmed around sideways on the seat and drew up her knees, making no attempt to conceal her legs. "Look, big boy," she said. "You and I might just as well get along. It'll be easier that way."

Bedford said nothing.

She made a little grimace at his silence and said, "I like to be sociable."

Then after a moment she straightened in the seat, pulled her skirt back down over her knees and said, "Okay, be grumpy if you want to. Turn left at the next corner, grouch-face."

He turned left at the next corner.

"Turn right on the freeway and go north," she instructed.

Bedford eased his way into the freeway traffic, instinctively looked at the gasoline gauge. It was full. He settled down for a long drive.

"Turn right again and leave the freeway up here at the next crossroads," she said.

Bedford followed instructions. Again the blonde doubled her knees up on the seat and rested one hand lightly on his shoulder.

Bedford realized then that she was carefully regarding the traffic behind them through the rear window of the car.

Bedford raised his eyes to the rearview mirror.

A single car followed them off the freeway, maintaining a respectable distance behind.

"Turn right," Geraldine said.

Bedford had a glimpse of the driver of that other car. It was Binney Denham.

From that point on Geraldine, seated beside him, gave a series of directions which sent him twisting and turning through traffic.

Always behind them was that single car, sometimes close, sometimes dropping far behind, until finally, apparently satisfied that no one was following them, the car disappeared and Geraldine Corning said, "All right, now we drive straight ahead. I'll tell you where to stop."

They followed the stream of traffic out Wilshire. At length, following her directions, he turned north.

"Slow down," she said.

Bedford slowed the car.

"Look for a good motel," she told him. "This is far enough."

As she spoke, they passed a motel on the left, but it was so shabby Bedford drove on without pausing. There was another motel half a mile ahead. It was named The Staylonger.

"How's this?" Bedford asked.

"I guess this will do. Turn in here. We get a motel unit and wait."

"How do I register?" Bedford asked.

She shrugged her shoulders. "I'm to keep you occupied until the thing is all over. Binney thought you'd be less nervous if you had me for company."

"Look here," Bedford said. "I'm a married man. I'm not going to get into any damned trap over this thing."

"Have it your way," she said. "We just wait here, that's all. There isn't any trap. Let your conscience be your guide."

Bedford entered the place. The manager smiled at him, showing gold teeth. He asked no questions.

Bedford signed the name, "S. G. Wilfred," and gave a San Diego address. At the same time he gave the story that he had hurriedly thought up. "We're to be joined by some friends who are driving in from San Diego. We got here early. Do you have a double cabin?"

"Sure we do," the manager said. "In fact, we have anything you want."

"I want a double."

"If you register for a double, you'll have to pay for both cabins. If you take a single, I'll reserve the other cabin until six o'clock and then your friends can register and pay."

"No, I'll pay for the whole business," Bedford said.

"That'll be twenty-eight dollars."

Bedford started to protest at the price; then, looking out at the young blonde sitting in the car, realized that it would be better to say nothing. He put twenty-eight dollars on the counter and received two keys.

"They're the two cabins down at the end with the double garage in between—numbers fifteen and sixteen. There's a connecting door," the manager said.

Bedford thanked him, went back to the car, drove it down, parked it in the garage and said, "Now what?"

"I guess we wait," Gerry told him.

Bedford unlocked one of the cabins and held the door open. She walked in. Bedford followed her.

It was a nice motel—a double bed, a little kitchenette, a refrigerator, and a connecting door between that and another unit that was exactly the same. There was also a toilet and tiled shower in each unit.

"Expecting company?" Geraldine asked.

"That's your room," Bedford said. "This one is mine."

She looked at him almost scornfully, then said, "Got the traveler's checks?"

Bedford nodded. She indicated the table and said, "You'd better start signing."

Bedford zipped open his brief case and was reaching for the traveler's checks when he saw the gun. He had forgotten about that. He hurriedly turned the brief case so she couldn't see in it and took out the books of traveler's checks.

He sat at the table and started signing the checks.

She slipped out of her jacket, looked at herself appraisingly in the mirror, studied her legs, straightened her stockings, glanced over her shoulder at Bedford and said, "I think I'll freshen up a bit."

She went through the connecting door into the other unit. Bedford heard the sound of running water. He heard a door close, a drawer open and close, then the outer door opened.

Suddenly suspicious, Bedford put down his pen, walked through the door and into the other room.

Geraldine was standing in her bra, panties and stockings in front of an open suitcase.

She turned casually and raised her eyebrows. "All signed so soon?" she asked.

"No," Bedford said angrily. "I heard a door open and close. I was wondering if you were taking a powder."

She laughed. "Just getting my suitcase out of the trunk compartment of the car," she said. "I'm not leaving you. You'd better go on with your signing. They'll want the checks pretty quick."

There was neither invitation nor embarrassment in her manner. She stood there watching him speculatively, and Bedford, annoyed at finding himself not only aware but warmly appreciative of her figure, turned back to his own unit in the motel and gave himself over to signing checks. For the second time that day he signed his name two hundred times, then went to the half-opened connecting door. "Everybody decent?" he asked.

"Oh, don't be so stuffy. Come on in," she said.

He entered the room to find Geraldine attired in a neat-fitting gabardine skirt which snugly outlined the curves of her hips, a soft pink sweater which clung to her ample breasts, and an expensive wide contour belt around her tiny waist.

"You have them?" she asked.

Bedford handed her the checks.

She took the books, carefully looked through each check to make sure that it was properly signed, glanced at her wrist watch and said, "I'm going out to the car for a minute. You stay here."

She went out, locking the door from the outside, leaving Bedford alone in the motel. Bedford whipped out a notebook, wrote the telephone number of his unlisted line, which connected directly with Elsa Griffin's desk. He wrote, "Call this number and say I am at The Staylonger Motel." He pulled a twenty-dollar bill from his billfold, doubled it over, with the leaf from his notebook inside, then folded the twenty-dollar bill again and thrust it in his vest pocket. He went to her suitcase, tried to learn something of her identity from an inspection of the contents.

The suitcase and the overnight bag beside it were brand new. The initials G. C. were stamped in gold on the leather. There were no other distinguishing marks.

He heard her step on the wooden stair outside the door and quietly withdrew from the vicinity of the baggage.

A moment later the girl opened the door. "I've got a bottle," she said. "How about a highball?"

"Too early in the day for me."

She lit a cigarette, stretched languidly, moved over to the bed and sat down. "We're going to have to wait quite a while," she said by way of explanation.

"For what?"

"To make sure everything clears, silly. You're not to go out—except with me. We stay here."

"When can I get back to my business?"

"Whenever everything's cleared. Don't be so impatient."

Bedford marched back into the other unit of the motel and sat down in a chair that was only fairly comfortable. Minutes seemed to drag into hours. At length he got up and walked back to the other unit. Geraldine was stretched out in the overstuffed chair. She had drawn up another chair to use as a footrest and the short skirt had slid back to show very attractive legs.

"I just can't sit here all day doing nothing," he said angrily.

"You want this thing to go through, don't you?"

"Of course I want it to go through; otherwise I wouldn't have gone this far. But after all, there are certain things that I don't intend to put up with."

"Come on, grumpy," she said. "Why not be human?

We're going to be here a while. Know anything about cards?"

"A little."

"How about gin rummy?"

"Okay," he said. "What do we play for?"

"Anything you want."

Bedford hesitated a moment, then made it a cent a point.

At the end of an hour he had lost twenty-seven dollars. He paused in his deal and said, "For heaven's sake, let's cut out this beating around the bush. *When* do I get out of here?"

"Sometime this afternoon, after the banks close."

"Now wait a minute!" he said. "That's going too damned far."

"Forget it," she told him. "Why don't you loosen up and be yourself? After all, I'm as human as you are. I get bored the same as you do. You're already parted with your money. You have everything to lose and nothing to gain by trying to crab the deal now. Sit down and relax. Take your coat off. Take your shoes off. Why don't you have a drink?"

She went over to the refrigerator, opened the door of the freezing compartment and took out a tray of ice cubes.

"Okay," Bedford surrendered. "What do you have?"

"Scotch on the rocks, or Scotch and water."

"Scotch on the rocks," he said.

"That's better," she told him. "I could like you if you weren't so grouchy. Lots of people would like to spend time here with me. We could have fun if you'd quit grinding your teeth. Know any funny stories?"

"They don't seem funny now," he said.

She opened a new fifth of Scotch, poured out generous drinks, looked at him over the brim of the glass, said, "Here's looking at you, big boy."

"Here's to crime!" Bedford said.

"That's better," she told him.

Bedford decided to try a new conversational gambit.

"You know," he told her, "you're quite an attractive girl. You certainly have a figure."

"I noticed you looking it over."

"You didn't seem very much concerned at the . . . at the lack of . . . of your costume."

"I've been looked at before."

"What do you do?" Bedford asked. "I mean, how do you make a living?"

"Mostly," she said, smiling, "I follow instructions."

"Who gives the instructions?"

"That," she said, "depends."

"Do you know this man they call Delbert?"

"Just by name."

"What kind of a man is he?"

"All I know is what Binney tells me. I guess he's a screwball . . . but smart. He's nervous—you know, jumpy."

"And you know Binney?"

"Oh, sure."

"What about Binney?"

"He's nice, in a mild sort of way."

"Well," he said, "let's get on some ground we can talk about. What did you do before you met that character?"

"Corespondent," she said.

"You mean, a professional corespondent?"

"That's right. Go to a hotel with a man, take my clothes off, wait for the raiding party."

"I didn't know they did that any more."

"It wasn't in this state."

"Where was it?"

"Some place else."

"You're not very communicative."

"Why not talk about you?" she said. "Tell me about your business."

"It's rather complicated," he explained.

She yawned. "You're determinedly virtuous, aren't you?"

"I'm married."

"Let's play some more cards."

They played cards until Geraldine decided she wanted to take a nap. She was pulling a zipper on her skirt as Bedford started for the connecting door.

"That's not nice," she said. "I have to be sure you don't go out."

"Are you going to lock the door?"

"It's locked."

"It is?"

"Sure," she said nonchalantly. "I have the keys. I locked it from the outside while I was out at the car. You didn't think I was dumb, did you?"

"I didn't know."

"Don't you ever take a nap?"

"Not in the daytime."

"Okay. I guess we'll have to suffer it out then. More cards or more Scotch—or both?"

"Don't you have a magazine?"

"You've got me. They didn't think you needed anything else to keep you entertained. After all, there are some details they couldn't have anticipated," she laughed.

Bedford went into his room and sat down. She followed him. After a while Bedford became drowsy with the sheer monotony of doing nothing. He stretched out on the bed. Then he dozed lightly, slept for a few minutes.

He wakened with the smell of seductive perfume in his nostrils. The blonde, wearing a loose-flowing, semi-transparent creation, was standing beside him, looking down at him, holding a small slip of paper.

Bedford wakened with a start. "What is it?" he asked.

"A message," she said. "There's been a hitch. We're going to be delayed."

"How long?"

"They didn't say."

"We have to eat," Bedford said.

"They've thought of that. We can go out and eat. I pick the place. You stay with me—all the time. No phones. If you want to powder your nose, do it before we start. If there's any double cross, you've just lost your money and Delbert goes to the magazine. I'm to tell you that. You're to do as I say.

"They want you to be contented and not be nervous. They thought I could keep you amused. I told them you don't amuse very easy, so they said I could take you out—but no phones."

"How did you communicate with them?" he asked.

She grinned. "Carrier pigeons. I have them in my bra. Didn't you see them?"

"All right. Let's ride around a while," he said. "Let's eat."

He was surprised to find himself experiencing a feeling of companionship as she slid in the car beside him. She twisted around to draw up her knees so that her right knee was resting across the edge of his leg. Her hands with fingers interlaced were on his shoulder.

"Hello, good-looking," she said.

"Hello, blonde," he told her.

Bedford drove down to the beach highway, drove slowly along, keeping to the outside of the road.

"Well," he said at length, "I suppose you're getting hungry."

"Thanks," she said.

He raised his eyebrows in silent interrogation.

"You're thinking of me as a human being," she explained. "After all, I am, you know."

"How did you get in this work?" he asked abruptly.

"It depends on what you mean by 'this work,' " she said.

There was a moment's silence. Bedford thought of two or three possible explanations which would elaborate on his remark, and decided against all of them.

After a moment she said, "I guess you just drift into things in life. Once you start drifting the current keeps moving more and more swiftly, until you just can't find the opportunity to turn and row against it. Now, I suppose that's being philosophical, and you don't expect that from me."

"I don't know what I am supposed to expect from you."

"Expect anything you want," she said. "They can't arrest you for expecting."

Bedford was thoughtful. "Why start drifting in the first place?" he asked.

"Because you don't realize there's any current, and even when you do, you like it better than sitting still. Damn it, I'm not going to give you a lot of philosophy on an empty stomach."

"There's a place here where they have wonderful steaks," Bedford said, starting to pull in and then suddenly changing his mind.

He looked up to see her eyes mildly amused, partially contemptuous, studying his features. "You're known there, eh?" she asked.

"I've been there."

"One look at me and your reputation is ruined, is that it?"

"No, that's *not* it," he said savagely. "And you should know that's not it. But under the circumstances, I'm not anxious to leave a broad back trail. I don't know who I'm playing with or what I'm playing with."

"You're sure not playing with me," she said. "And remember, I'm to pick the eating place. You pay the check."

He drove up the road for a couple of miles. "Try this one," she said abruptly, indicating a tavern.

They found a booth in a dining room that was built out over the water. The air was balmy, the sun warm, the ocean had a salty tang, and they ate thick filet mignon steaks with French-fried onions, Guinness stout, and garlic bread.

35

They had dessert, a brandy and Benedictine, and Bedford paid the check. "And this is for you," he told the waiter, handing him the folded twenty with the message inside.

He scraped back his chair, careful to have Geraldine on her way to the door before the waiter unfolded the bill. He knew he was being foolish, jeopardizing the twenty thousand dollar investment he had made in a blackmail payoff, but he had the feeling he was outwitting his enemies.

Only afterward, when they had again started driving up the coast road, did he regret his action. After all, it could do no good and it might do harm, might, in fact, wreck everything.

Yet his reason told him they weren't going to any scandal magazine, not when they had a bonanza that could be clipped for twenty thousand dollars at a crack.

And the more he thought of it, the more he felt certain Delbert was only a fictitious figment. Binney Denham and the blonde were all there were in the "gang."

Was it perhaps possible that this acquiescent blonde was the brains of the gang? Yet now, somehow, he accepted her as a fellow human being. He preferred to regard her as a good scout who had somehow come under the power of Binney, a sinister individual beneath his apologetic mask.

The silence between Bedford and the girl was warm and intimate.

"You're a good guy," she told him, "when a girl gets to know you. You're a shock to a girl's vanity at first. I guess some married men are like that and are all wrapped up in their wives."

"Thanks," he told her. "You're a good scout yourself, when a fellow gets to know you."

"How long you been married?"

"Nearly two years."

"Happy?"

"Uh-huh."

"This deal you're mixed up in involves her, doesn't it?"

"If it's all the same with you, I'd rather not talk about her."

"Okay by me. We probably should be getting back."

"They'll let you know when everything is clear?"

"Uh-huh. It takes a little time to negotiate two hundred traveler's checks, you know, and do it right."

"And you're supposed to keep me out of circulation until it's done right, is that it?"

Her eyes flickered over him slowly. "Something like that," she said.

"Why didn't Binney do the job?"

"They thought you might get impatient with him."

"They?" he asked.

"Me and my big mouth," she told him. "Let's talk about politics or sex or business statistics, or something that I can agree with you on."

"You think you could agree with me on politics?"

"Sure, I'm broad-minded. You know something?"

"What?"

"I'd like a drink."

"We can stop in one of these roadhouses," Bedford suggested.

She shook her head. "They might not like that. Let's go back to the motel. I'm not to let you out of my sight, and I'm going to have to powder my nose. How'd you happen to get mixed up in a mess of this sort?"

"Let's not talk about it," he said.

"Okay. Drive back. I guess you just drifted into it the same way I did. They start telling you what to do, and you give in. After the first time it's harder to resist. I know it was with me. But you have to turn against the current sometime. I guess the best time is when you first feel the current.

"I'm spilling to you. I shouldn't. It's not in the job.

37

They wouldn't like it. I guess it's because you're so damned decent. I guess you've always been a square shooter.

"You take me, I've always gone along the easy way. I guess I haven't guts enough to stand up and face things."

They drove in silence for a while. At length she said, "There's only one way out."

"For whom?"

"For both of us. I'd forgotten how damned decent a decent guy could be."

"What's the way out?" he asked.

She shook her head, became suddenly silent.

She cuddled a little closer to him. Bedford's mind, which had been working furiously, began to relax. After all, he had been a fool, putting himself in the power of Binney Denham and the mysterious individual whom he knew only as Delbert. They had his money. They wouldn't want any publicity now. Probably they'd play fair with him because they'd want to put the bite on him again—and again and again.

Bedford knew he was going to have to do something about that, but there would be a respite now, a period of time during which he'd have an opportunity to plan some sort of attack.

Bedford turned in at the motel. The manager looked out of the door to see who it was, apparently recognized the car, waved a salutation, and turned back from the window.

Bedford drove into the garage. Geraldine Corning, who had both keys, unlocked the door and entered his cabin with him. She got the bottle of Scotch, took the deck of cards, suddenly laughed and threw the cards in the wastebasket. "Let's try getting along without these things. I was never so bored in my life. That's a hell of a way to make money."

She went to the refrigerator, got out ice cubes, put them

in the glasses, poured him a drink, then poured herself one.

She went to the kitchenette, added a little water to each drink, came back with a spoon and stirred them. She touched the rim of her glass to his and said, "Here's to crime!"

They sat sipping their drinks.

Geraldine kicked her shoes off, ran the tips of her fingers up her stockings, looked at her leg, quite plainly admiring it, stretched, yawned, sipped the drink again and said, "I feel sleepy."

She stretched out a stockinged foot, hooked it under the rung of one of the straight-backed chairs, dragged it toward her, propped her feet up and tilted back in the overstuffed chair.

"You know," she said, "there are times in a girl's life when she comes to a fork in the road, and it all happens so easily and naturally that she doesn't realize she's coming to a crisis."

"Meaning what?" Bedford asked.

"What do they call you?" she asked. "Your friends . . ."

"My first name's Stewart."

"That's a helluva name," she said. "Do they call you Stu?"

"Uh-huh."

"All right, I'll call you Stu. Look Stu, you've shown me something."

"What?"

"You've shown me that you can't get anywhere drifting. I'm either going to turn back or head for shore," she said. "I'm damned sick and tired of letting people run my life. Tell me something about your wife."

Bedford stretched out on the bed and dropped both pillows behind his head. "Let's not talk about her."

"You mean you don't want to discuss her with *me?*"

"Not exactly."

"What I wanted to know," Geraldine said somewhat

wistfully, "was what kind of a woman it is who can make a man love her the way you do."

"She's a very wonderful girl," Bedford said.

"Hell! I know *that*. Don't waste time telling me about that. I want to know how she reacts toward life and . . . and somehow I'd like to know what it is that Binney has on her."

"Why?"

"Damned if I know," she said. "I thought I might be able to help her." She put back her head and sucked in air in a prodigious yawn. "Cripes! but I'm sleepy!"

For some time there was silence. Bedford put his head back against the pillows and found himself thinking about Ann Roann. He felt somehow that he should tell Geraldine something about her, something about her vitality, her personality, her knack of saying witty things that were never unkind.

Bedford heard a gentle sigh and looked over to see that Geraldine had fallen asleep. He himself felt strangely drowsy. He began to relax in a way that was most unusual considering the circumstances. The nervous tension drained out of him. His eyes closed, then opened, and for a moment he saw double. It took him a conscious effort to fuse the two images into one.

He sat up and was suddenly dizzy, then dropped back against the pillows. He knew then that the drink had been drugged. By that time it was too late to do anything about it. He made a halfhearted effort to get up off the bed, but lacked the energy to do it. He surrendered to the warm feeling of drowsiness that was sweeping over him.

He thought he heard voices. Someone was saying something in whispers, something that concerned him. He thought he heard the rustle of paper. He knew that this had something to do with some responsibility of his in the waking world. He tried to arouse himself to cope with that responsibility, but the drug was too strong within him and the warm silence enveloped him.

He heard the sound of a motor, and then the motor backfired and again he tried to arouse from a lethargy. He was unable to do so.

What seemed like an eternity later Bedford began to regain consciousness. He was, he knew, stretched out on a bed in a motel. He should get up. There was a girl in the room. She had drugged his drink. He thought that over with his eyes closed for what seemed like ten or fifteen minutes, thinking for a moment, then dozing, then waking to think again. *His* drink had been drugged, but the *girl's* drink must have also been drugged. They had been out somewhere. She had left the bottle in the room. Someone must have entered the room and drugged the bottle of whisky while they were out. She was a nice girl. He had hated her at first, but she had a lot of good in her after all. She liked him. She wouldn't have resented his making a pass at her. In fact, she resented it because he hadn't. It had been a blow to her vanity. Then it had started her thinking, started her thinking about his wife. She had wanted to know about Ann Roann.

The thought of Ann Roann snapped his eyes open.

There was no light in the room except that which came through the adjoining door from the other unit in the motel unit hurt his eyes momentarily. He started to get up and became conscious of a piece of paper pinned to his left coat sleeve. He turned the paper so that the light struck it. He read: "Everything has cleared. You can go now. Love, Gerry."

Bedford struggled to a sitting position.

He walked toward the lighted door of the adjoining unit of the motel, his eyes rapidly becoming accustomed to the brighter light from the interior of the room. He started to call out, "Everybody decent?" and then thought better of it. After all, Geraldine would have left the door closed if she had cared. There was a friendly warmth about her, and, thinking of her, Bedford felt suddenly very kindly. He remembered when he had gone through that door earlier and had found her standing there practically nude. She really had an unusually beautiful figure. He had kept staring at her and she had merely stared back with an expression of amused tolerance. She had made no attempt to reach for her robe or turn her back. She had just stood there.

Bedford stepped into the room.

The first thing he saw was the figure lying on its side on the floor, the red pool which had spread out onto the carpet, the surface glazed over and reflecting the light from the reading lamp in a reddish splotch against the wall.

The figure was that of Binney Denham, and the little man was quite dead. Even in death he seemed to be apologetic. It was as though he was protesting against the necessity of staining the faded rug with the pool of red which had flowed from his chest.

■ 4 ■

FOR A MOMENT PANIC GRIPPED STEWART BEDFORD. HE hurried back to the other room, found his hat and his brief case. He opened the brief case, looked for his gun. The gun was gone.

He put on his hat, held the brief case in his hand, closed the door into the adjoining unit, and by so doing shut out all of the light except a flickering red illumination which came and went at regular intervals.

Bedford pulled aside the curtain, looked out and saw that this light came from a large red sign which flashed on and off the words *The Staylonger Motel,* and down below that a crimson sign which glowed steadily, reading *Vacancy*.

Bedford tried the door of the motel, shuddering at the thought that perhaps Geraldine had left the door locked from the outside. However, the door was unlocked, the knob turned readily, and the door swung open.

Bedford looked out into the lighted courtyard. The units of the motel were arranged in the shape of a big *U*. There were lights on over each doorway and each garage, giving the motel an appearance of great depth.

Bedford looked in the garage between the two units which he and Geraldine had been occupying. The garage was empty. The yellow car was gone.

Faced with the problem of getting out where he could find a taxicab, Stewart Bedford realized that he simply lacked the courage to walk down the length of that lighted central yard. The office was at the far end, right next to the street. The manager would be almost certain to see him walking out and might ask questions.

Bedford closed the door of unit fifteen, walked rapidly around the side of the building until he came to the end of the motel lot. There was a barbed wire fence here, and Bedford slid his brief case through to the other side, then tried to ease himself between the wires. These barbed wires were tightly strung; Bedford was nervous, and just as he thought he was safely through, he caught the knee of the trousers and felt the cloth rip slightly.

Then he was free and walking across the uneven surface of a field. The light from the motel sign behind him gave him enough illumination so he could avoid the pitfalls.

He found himself on a side road which led toward the main highway, along which there was a steady stream of automobiles coming and going in both directions.

Bedford walked rapidly along this road.

A car coming along the main highway slowed, then suddenly turned down the side road. Bedford found him-

43

self caught in the glare of the headlights. For a moment he was gripped with panic and wanted to resort to flight. Then he realized that his would be a suspicious circumstance which might well be communicated to the police and result in a prowl car exploring the territory. He elevated his chin, squared his shoulders, and walked steadily along the side of the road toward the headlights, trying to walk purposefully as though going on some mission—a businessman with a brief case walking to keep some appointment at a neighboring establishment.

The headlights grew brighter. The car swerved and came to a stop abreast of Bedford. He heard the door open.

"Stu! Oh, Stu!" Elsa Griffin's voice called.

She was, he saw, half-hysterical with apprehension, and in the flood of relief which came over him at the sound of her voice he didn't notice that it was the first time in over five years she had called him by his familiar nickname.

"Get in, get in," she said, and Stewart Bedford slid into the car.

"What happened?" she asked.

"I don't know," Bedford said. "All sorts of things. I'm afraid we're in trouble. How did *you* get here?"

"Your telephone message," she said. "Someone who said he was a waiter telephoned that a man had left a message and a twenty-dollar—"

"Yes, yes," he interrupted. "What did you do?"

She said, "I went down to the motel and rented a unit. I used an assumed name and a fictitious address. I juggled the figures on my license, and the manager never noticed. I spotted that yellow car—I'd already checked the license. It was a rented car from one of the drive-yourself agencies."

"So what did you do?" he asked.

"I sat and watched and watched and watched," she said. "Of course I couldn't sit right in the doorway and

44

keep my eye on the cabin, but I sat back and had my door open so that if anyone came or went from that cabin I would see it, and if the car drove out I could be all ready to follow."

"Go on," he said. "What happened?"

"Well," she said, "about an hour and a half ago the car backed out and turned."

"What did you do?"

"I jumped in my car and followed. Of course, not too close, but I was close enough so that after the car got on the highway I could easily keep behind it. I had gone a couple of miles before I dared draw close enough to see that this blonde girl was alone in my car. I turned around and came back and parked my car. And believe me, I've had the devil of an hour. I didn't know whether you were all right or not. I wanted to go over there, and yet I was afraid to. I found that by standing in the bathroom, with the window open, I could look out and see the garage door and the door of the two units down there at the end. So I stood there in the bathroom watching. And then I saw you come out and go around the back of the house. I thought perhaps you were coming around toward the street by the back of the houses. When you didn't show up, I realized you must have gone through the fence, so I jumped in my car and drove around, and when I came to this cross street I turned down it and there you were."

"Things are in quite a mess, Elsa," he said. "There's somebody dead in that cabin."

"Who?"

"Binney Denham."

"How did it happen?"

"I'm afraid he was shot," he said. "And we may be in trouble. I put my gun in my brief case when I got that phone call last night. I had it with me."

"Oh, I was afraid," she said. "I was afraid something like that might happen."

"Now wait a minute," Bedford said. "*I* didn't kill him. I don't know anything about it. I was asleep. The girl gave me a drugged drink—I don't think it was her fault. I think someone got into the cabin and drugged the whole bottle of whisky. She poured drinks out of that."

"Well," Elsa Griffin said, "I have Perry Mason, the lawyer, waiting in his office."

"The devil you have!" he exclaimed in surprise.

She nodded.

"How come you did that?"

She said, "I just had a feeling in my bones. I knew there was something wrong. I rang Mr. Mason shortly after you left the office and told him that you were in trouble, that I couldn't discuss it, but I wanted to know where I could reach him at any hour of the day or night. Of course, he's done enough work for you so he feels you're a regular client and . . . well, he gave me a number and I called it about an hour ago, right after I returned from chasing that blonde. I had a feeling something was wrong. I told him to wait at his office until he heard from me. I told him that it would be all right to send you a bill for whatever it was worth, but I wanted him there."

Stewart Bedford reached out and patted her shoulder. "The perfect secretary!" he said. "Let's go."

■ 5 ■

IT WAS AFTER TEN O'CLOCK. PERRY MASON, THE FAMOUS trial lawyer, sat in his office. Della Street, his trusted confidential secretary, occupied the easy chair on the other side of the desk.

Mason looked at his watch and said, "We'll give them until eleven and then go home."

"You talked with Stewart G. Bedford's secretary?"

"That's right."

"I take it it's terribly important?"

"She said money was no object, that Mr. Bedford had to see me tonight, but that she would have to get hold of him before she could bring him up here."

"That sounds strange."

"Uh-huh."

"He married about two years ago, didn't he?"

"I believe so."

"Do you know his secretary?"

"I've met her three or four times. Quite a girl. Loyal, quiet, reserved, efficient. Wait a minute, Della, here's someone now."

Knuckles tapped gently at the heavy corridor door from the private office.

Della Street opened it.

Elsa Griffin and Stewart Bedford entered the office.

"Thank heaven you're still here!" Elsa Griffin said. "We got here as fast as we could."

"What's the trouble, Bedford?" Mason asked, shaking hands. "I guess both of you know my secretary, Della Street. What's it all about?"

"I don't think it's anything to worry about," Bedford said, making an obvious effort to be cheerful.

"I do," Elsa Griffin said. "They can trace S. G. through the traveler's checks."

Mason indicated chairs. "Suppose you sit down and tell me about it from the beginning."

Bedford said, "I had a business deal with a man whom I know as Binney Denham. That may not be his name. He seems to have got himself murdered down in a motel this evening."

"Do the police know about it?"

"Not yet."

"Murdered?"

"Yes."

"How do you know?"

"He saw the body," Elsa Griffin said.

"Notify anyone?" Mason asked.

Bedford shook his head.

"We thought we'd better see you," Elsa Briffin said.

"What was the business deal?" Mason asked.

"A private matter," Bedford explained.

"What was the business deal?" Mason repeated.

"I tell you it's just a private matter. Now that Denham is dead there's no reason for anyone to—"

"What was the business deal?" Mason asked.

"Blackmail," Elsa Griffin said.

"I thought so," Mason said grimly. "Let's have the story. Don't hold anything back. I want it all."

"Tell him, S. G.," Elsa Griffin said, "or I will."

Bedford frowned, thought for a moment, then told the story from the beginning. He even took out the police photograph of his wife and her description and fingerprints. "They left this with me," he explained, giving it to Mason.

Mason studied the card. "That's your wife?"

Bedford nodded.

"Of course you know it's her picture, but you can't tell about the fingerprints," Mason said. "After all, it may be a fake."

"No, they're her prints all right," Bedford said.

"How do you know?"

Bedford told him about the silver cocktail tray, the lifted fingerprints.

"You'll have to report the murder," Mason said.

"What happens if I don't?"

"Serious trouble," Mason said. "Miss Griffin, you go down to a pay station, call the police department, don't give them your name. Tell them there's a body down in unit sixteen at The Staylonger Motel."

"I'd better do it," Bedford said.

Mason shook his head. "I want a girl's voice to make the report."

"Why?"

"Because they'll find out a girl was in there."

"Then what do we do?" Bedford asked.

Mason looked at his watch, said, "I now have the job of getting Paul Drake of the Drake Detective Agency out of bed and on the job, and I can't put it on the line with him because I don't dare to let him know what he's investigating.

"What's the license number of that automobile?"

"It's a rented automobile from one of the drive-yourself agencies and—"

"What's the number?" Mason asked.

Elsa Griffin gave it to him. "License number CXY 221."

Mason called Paul Drake of the Drake Detective Agency at his unlisted number. After he heard Drake's sleepy voice on the line, he said, "Paul, here's a job that will require your personal attention."

"Good lord!" Drake protested. "Don't you *ever* sleep?"

Mason said, "Police are discovering a body at The Staylonger Motel, down by the beach. I want to know everything there is to know about the case."

"What do you mean, they are *discovering* a body?"

"Present participle," Mason said.

"Because minutes are precious," Mason told him. "Here's a car license number. It's probably a drive-yourself number. I want you to find out just where that car is, who rented it, and if it's been returned I want to know the exact time of its return. Now then, here's something else. I want you to get some operative who is really above suspicion, someone who can put on a front of being entirely, utterly innocent, preferably a woman. I want that woman to rent that car just as soon as it is available."

"What does she do with it after she rents it?"

"She drives it to some place where my criminalist can go over it with a vacuum sweeper, testing it for hairs, fibers, bloodstains, weapons, fingerprints."

"Then what?"

"Then," Mason said, "I want this woman to go up somewhere in the mountains first thing in the morning and get some topsoil for her garden, fill the car full of pasteboard boxes containing leaf mold, and pick up some frozen meat to take home to her locker."

"In other words," Drake said, "you want her to contaminate the hell out of any evidence that's left."

"Oh, nothing like that!" Mason said. "I wouldn't *think* of doing anything like that, Paul! After all, there wouldn't be anything left to contaminate. We'd have a criminalist pick up all of the evidence that was in it."

Drake thought that over. "Isn't it a crime to juggle evidence around?"

"Suppose the criminalist removed every bit of evidence *first?*"

"Then what do we do with the criminalist?"

"Let him report to the police if he wants," Mason said. "In that way we know what he knows first. Otherwise, the police know what's in the car, and we don't find out until the district attorney puts his expert on the stand as a witness."

"Then why all the leaf mold and frozen meat and stuff?" Drake asked.

"So some criminalist doesn't come up with soil samples, bloodstains and hairs, make a wild guess as to where they came from and testify to it as an expert," Mason told him.

Drake groaned. "Okay," he said wearily. "Here we go again. What criminalist do you want?"

"Try Dr. Leroy Shelby if you get hold of the car."

"Is he supposed to know what it's all about?"

"He's supposed to find every bit of evidence that's in that car," Mason said.

"Okay," Drake told him wearily. "I'll get busy."

"Now get this," Mason said. "We're one jump ahead of the police, perhaps just half a jump. They may have the license number of that automobile by morning. Get Dr. Shelby out of bed if you have to. I want all the evidence that's in that car carefully impounded."

"They'll ask Shelby who hired him."

"Sure they will. That's where you come in."

"Then they'll come down on me like a thousand bricks."

"What if they do?" Mason asked.

"Then what do I tell them?"

"Tell them I hired you."

There was relief in Drake's voice. "I can do that?"

"You can do that," Mason told him, "but get busy."

Mason hung up the phone, said to Bedford, "Your next job is to get home and try to convince your wife that you've been at a directors' meeting or a business conference, and make it sound convincing. Think you can do that?"

"If she's already gone to bed, perhaps I can," Bedford said. "She isn't as inquisitive when she's sleepy."

"You're to be congratulated," Mason told him drily. "Be available where I can call you in the morning. If anybody asks you any questions about anything at all, refer them to me. Now, probably someone will want to know about those traveler's checks. You tell them it was a business deal and that it's too confidential to be discussed with anyone. Refer them to me."

Bedford nodded.

"Think you can do that?" Mason asked.

"I can do it all right," Bedford said, and then added, "Whether I can get away with it or not is another question."

Bedford left the office. Elsa Griffin started to go with him, but Mason stopped her. "Give him a few minutes' head start," he said.

"What do I do after I have called the police?"

51

"For the moment," Mason told her, "you get out of circulation and keep out of circulation."

"Could I come back here?"

"Why?"

"I'm anxious to know what's going on. I would like to be on the firing line. You're going to wait here, aren't you?"

Mason nodded.

"I wouldn't be in the way and perhaps I could help you with telephone calls and things."

"Okay," Mason told her. "You know what to tell the police?"

"Just about the body."

"That's right."

"Then, of course, they'll want to know who's talking."

"Never mind what they want to know," Mason said. "Tell them about the body. If they interrupt you to ask you a question, don't let them pull that gag and get away with it. Keep right on talking. They'll listen when you start telling them about the body. As soon as you've told them that, hang up."

"Isn't that against the law?"

"What law?"

"Suppressing evidence?"

"What evidence?"

"Well, when a person finds a body . . . just to go away and say nothing about . . . about who you are—"

"Is your identity going to help them find the body?" Mason asked. "You can tell them where it is. That's what they're interested in. The body. But don't tell them who you are. You make a note of the time of the call."

"But how about withholding my name?"

"That," Mason told her, "is information which might tend to incriminate you. You don't have to give that to anyone, not even on the witness stand."

"Okay," she said. "I'll follow your instructions."

"Do that," Mason told her.

She closed the door behind her as she eased out into the corridor.

Della Street looked at Mason. "I presume we'll want some coffee?"

"Coffee, doughnuts, cheeseburgers, and potato chips," Mason said and then shuddered. "What an awful mess to put in your stomach this time of night."

Della Street smiled. "Now we know how Paul Drake feels. This time the situation is reversed. We're usually out eating steaks while Drake is in his office eating hamburgers."

"And sodium bicarb," Mason said.

"*And* sodium bicarb." She smiled. "I'll telephone the order for the food down to the lunch counter."

Mason said, "Get the Thermos jug out of the law library, Della. Have them fill that with coffee. We may be up all night."

■ 6 ■

AT ONE O'CLOCK IN THE MORNING PAUL DRAKE TAPPED his code knock on the hall door of Mason's private office.

Della Street let him in.

Paul Drake walked over to the client's big, overstuffed chair, slid into his favorite position with his knees over the arms and said, "I'm going to be in the office from now on, Perry. I've got men out working on all the angles. I thought you'd like to get the dope."

"Shoot," Mason said.

"First on the victim. His name is Binney Denham. No one seems to know what he does. He had a safe-deposit box in an all-night-and-day bank. The safe-deposit box was in joint tenancy with a fellow by the name of Harry Elston. At nine forty-five last night Elston showed up at the bank and went to the box. He was carrying a brief case with him. Nobody knows whether he put in or took out. Police have now sealed up the box. An inheritance tax appraiser is going to be on hand first thing in the morning and they'll open it up. Bet it'll be empty."

Mason nodded.

"Aside from that, you can't find out a thing. Denham has no bank account, left no trail in the financial world, yet he lived well, spent a reasonable amount of money, all in cash.

"Police are going to check and see if he made income-tax returns as soon as things open up in the morning.

"Now, in regard to that car. It was a drive-yourself car. I tried to get it, but police already had the license number. They telephoned in and the car is impounded."

"Who rented it, Paul?"

"A nondescript person with an Oklahoma driving license. The driving license data was on the rental contract. The police have checked and it doesn't mean a damned thing. Fictitious name. Fictitious address."

"Man or woman?"

"Mousy little man. No one seems to remember much about him."

"What else?"

"Down at the motor court, police have some pretty good description stuff. It seems that the two units were occupied by a man and a babe. The man claimed he was expecting another couple. They got a double unit, connecting door. The man registered; the girl sat in the car. The manager didn't get a very good look, but had the impression she was a blonde, with good skin, swell figure, and that indefinable something that marks the babe, the chick, the moll. The man looked just a little bit frightened. Businessman type. Got a good description of him."

"Shoot," Mason said.

"Fifty to fifty-four. Gray suit. Height five feet nine. Weight about a hundred and ninety or a hundred and ninety-five. Gray eyes. Rather long, straight nose. Mouth rather wide and determined. Wore a gray hat, but seemed to have plenty of hair, which wasn't white except a very slight bit of gray at the temples."

Elsa Griffin flashed Mason a startled glance at the accuracy of the description.

Mason's poker face warned her to silence.

"Anything else, Paul?" the lawyer asked.

"Yes. A girl showed up and rented unit number twleve—rather an attractive girl, dark, slender, quiet, thirty to thirty-five."

"Go ahead," Mason said.

"She registered; was in and out, is now out and hasn't returned as yet."

"How does she enter into the picture?" Mason asked.

"She's okay," Drake said. "But the manager says he caught a woman prowling her place—a woman about thirty, thirty-one, thirty-two. A swell-looker, striking figure, one of the long-legged, queenly sort; dark hair, gray eyes. She was prowling this unit twelve. The manager caught her coming out. She wasn't registered at the place and he wanted to know what she was doing. She told him she was supposed to meet her friend there, that the friend wasn't in; the door was unlocked, so she had gone in, sat down and waited for nearly an hour."

"Have any car?" Mason asked.

"That's the suspicious part of it. She must have parked her car a block or two away and walked back. She was on foot, but there's no bus line nearer than half a mile to the place, and this gal was all dolled up—high heels and everything."

"And she was prowling unit number twelve?"

"Yes, that's the only suspicious thing the manager noticed. It was around eight o'clock. The woman in unit twelve had just checked in two hours or so earlier, then had driven out.

"The manager took this other woman—the prowler—at face value; didn't think anything more about it. But when the police asked him to recall anything at all that was out of the ordinary, he recalled her.

"Police don't attach any significance to her . . . as yet anyway.

"The manager remembered seeing the yellow car go out somewhere around eight o'clock, he thinks it was, and, while he can't be positive, it's his impression the blonde girl was driving the car and no one else was in the car with her. That gave the police an idea that she *might* have left before the shooting took place. They can't be certain about the time of the shooting."

"It was a shooting?" Mason asked.

"That's right. One shot from a .38 caliber revolver. The guy was shot in the back. The bullet went through the heart and he died almost instantly."

"How do they know it was fired from the back?" Mason asked. "They haven't had an autopsy yet."

"They found the bullet," Drake said. "It went entirely through the body and failed to penetrate the front of the coat. The bullet rolled out when they moved the body. That happens a lot more frequently than you'd suppose. The powder charge in a .38 caliber cartridge is just about sufficient to take the bullet through a body, and if the clothes furnish resistance the bullet will be trapped."

"Then they have the fatal bullet?"

"That's right."

"What sort of shape is it in, do you know, Paul? Is it flattened out pretty bad, or is it—"

"No, it's in pretty good shape, as I understand it. The police are confident that there are enough individual markings so they can identify the gun if and when they find it.

"Now, let me go on, Perry. They got the idea that if the blonde took out alone it might have been because this man Denham showed up and he was having an argument with her boy friend. He used the name of S. G. Wilfred when he registered and gave a San Diego address. The address is phony and the name seems to be fictitious."

"Okay, go ahead. What happened?"

"Well, the police got the idea that if this man, whom we'll call Wilfred, had popped Denham in a fight over the gal and then was left without a car there at the motel, he might have tried to sneak out the back way. So they started looking for tracks, and sure enough, they found where he had gone through a barbed wire fence and evidently snagged his clothes. The police got a few clothing fibers from the barbed wire where he went through— that was clever work. Your friend, Lieutenant Tragg, was on the job, and as soon as he saw the tracks going through the barbed wire he started using a magnifying glass. Sure enough, he caught some fibers on the barbed wire."

"What about the tracks?" Mason asked.

"They've having a moulage made of the footprints. They followed the tracks through the wire, across a field and out to a side road. They have an idea the man probably walked down to the main highway and hitchhiked his way into town. The police will be broadcasting an appeal in the newspapers, asking for anyone who noticed a hitchhiker to give a description."

"I see," Mason said thoughtfully. "What else, Paul?"

"Well, that car was returned to the rental agency. A young woman put the car in the agency parking lot, started toward the office and then seems to have disappeared. Of course, you know how these things go. The person who rents the car puts up a fifty-dollar deposit, and the car rental people don't worry about cars that are brought in. Its up to the renter to check in at the office in order to get the deposit back. The rental and mileage on a daily basis don't ordinarily run up to fifty bucks."

"The police have taken charge of the car?"

"That's right. They've had a fingerprint man on it, and

I understand there are some pretty good fingerprints. Of course, they're fingerprinting units fifteen and sixteen down there at the motel."

"Well," Mason said, "they'll probably have something pretty definite then."

"Hell! They've got something pretty definite right now," Drake said. "The only thing they *haven't* got is the man who matches the fingerprints. But don't overlook any bets on that. They'll have him, Perry."

"When?"

Drake lowered his eyes in thoughtful contemplation of the problem. "Even money they have him by ten o'clock in the morning," he said, "and I'd give you big odds they have him by five o'clock in the afternoon."

"What are you going to do now?" Mason asked.

"I have a couch in one of the offices. I'm going to get a little shut-eye. I've got operatives crawling all over the place, picking up all the leads they can."

"Okay," Mason said. "If anything happens, get in touch with me."

"Where will you be?"

"Right here."

Drake said, "You must have one hell of an important client in this case."

"Don't do any speculating," Mason told him. "Just keep information coming in."

"Thanks for the tip," Drake told him and walked out.

Mason turned to Elsa Griffin. "Apparently," he said, "no one has attached the slightest suspicion to you."

"That was a very good description of the occupant of unit twelve," she said.

"Want to go back?" Mason asked.

There was a sudden, swift alarm in her face.

"Go back? What for?"

Mason said, "As you know, Bedford told me about your help in getting the fingerprints off that silver platter. How would you like to go back down to the motel, drive

58

in to your place at unit twelve. The manager will probably come over to see if you're all right. You can give him a song and dance, then take a fingerprint outfit and go to work on the doorknobs, on the drawers in the dresser, any place where someone would be apt to have left fingerprints. Lift those fingerprints with tape and bring them back to me."

"But suppose . . . suppose the manager is suspicious. Suppose he rechecks my license number. I juggled the figures when I gave him the license number of the car when I registered."

"That," Mason said, "is a chance we'll have to take."

She shook her head. "That wouldn't be fair to Mr. Bedford. If anybody identified me, the trail would lead directly to him."

"There are too damn many trails leading directly to him the way it is," Mason told her. "Paul Drake was right. It's even money they'll have him by ten o'clock in the morning. In any event, they'll have him by five o'clock in the afternoon. He left two hundred traveler's checks scattered around, and Binney Denham was getting the money on those checks. Police will start backtracking Denham during the day. They'll find out where some of those checks were cashed. Then the trail will lead directly to Bedford. They'll match his fingerprints."

"And then what?" she asked.

"Then," Mason told her, "we have a murder case to try. Then we go to court."

"And then what?"

"Then they have to prove him guilty beyond all reasonable doubt. Do you think he killed Denham?"

"No!" she said with sudden vehemence.

"All right," Mason said, "he has his story. He has the note that was pinned to his sleeve, the note he found when he woke up saying he could leave."

"But what reason does he give for not reporting the body?"

"He did report the body," Mason said. "You reported it. *He* told you to telephone the police. He did everything he could to start the police on their investigation, but he just tried to keep his name out of it. It was an ill-advised attempt to avoid publicity because he was dealing with a blackmailer."

She thought it over for a while and said, "Mr. Bedford isn't going to like that."

"What isn't he going to like about it?"

"Having to explain to the police why he was down there."

"He doesn't have to explain anything," Mason said. "He can keep silent. *I'll* do the talking."

"I'm afraid he won't like that either."

Mason said impatiently, "There's going to be a lot about this he won't like before he gets done. Persons who are accused of murder seldom like the things the police do in connection with developing the case."

"He'll be accused of murder?"

"Can you think of any good reason why he won't?"

"You think I can do some real good by going down and looking for fingerprints?"

Mason said, "It's a gamble. From what Drake tells me, you're apparently not involved in any way. The manager of the motel won't want to have his guests annoyed. He'll keep the trouble centralized in cabins fifteen and sixteen as far as possible. You have a cocktail and spill a little on a scarf you'll have around your neck so it will be obvious you've been drinking. Go into the motel just as though nothing had happened. If the manager comes over to you about a prowler in your cabin, tell him the woman was perfectly all right, that she was a friend of yours who was coming to visit you, that you told her to go in and wait in case you weren't there, that you got tied up on a date with someone you liked very much and had to stand her up.

"I'd like to have the fingerprints of whoever it was

that was in that cabin, but what I'd mainly like is to have *you* remove all of *your* fingerprints. After you get done developing latent prints and lifting any that you find, take some soap and warm water and scrub the place all to pieces. Get rid of anything incriminating."

"Why?" she asked.

"Because," Mason said, "if later on the police get the idea that there's something funny about the occupant of unit number twelve and start looking for fingerprints, they won't find yours.

"Don't you see the thing that's going to attract suspicion to you above all else is *not* going back there tonight? If your cabin isn't occupied, the manager will report that as another suspicious circumstance to the police."

"Okay," she said. "I'm on my way. Where do I get the fingerprint outfit?"

Mason grinned. "We keep one here for emergencies. You know how to lift fingerprints all right. Bedford said you did it from that cocktail tray."

"I know how," she said. "Believe it or not, I took a correspondence course as a detective. I'm on my way."

"If anything happens," Mason warned, "anything at all, call Paul Drake's agency. I'll be in constant touch with Paul Drake. If anyone should start questioning you, dry up like a clam."

"On my way," she told him.

Seven o'clock found Paul Drake back in Perry Mason's office.

"What do you know about this Binney Denham, Perry?" the detective asked.

"What do *you* know about him?" Mason countered.

"Only what the police know. But it's beginning to pile up into something."

"Go on."

"Well, he had the lock box in joint tenancy with Harry Elston. Elston went to the lock box, and now police can't find him. That's to have been expected. Police found where Binney Denham was living. It was a pretty swank apartment for one man who was supposedly living by himself."

"Why do you say supposedly?"

"Police think it was rather a convivial arrangement."

"What did they find?"

"Forty thousand dollars in cash neatly hidden under the carpet. Hundred dollar bills. A section of the carpet had been pulled up so many times that it was a dead giveaway. The floor underneath it was pretty well paved with hundred dollar bills."

"Income tax?" Mason asked.

"They haven't got at that yet. They'll enlist the aid of the income-tax boys this morning."

"Makes it nice," Mason said.

"Doesn't it," Paul Drake observed.

"What else do you know?"

"Police are acting on the theory that Binney Denham may have been mixed up in a blackmail racket and that he may have been killed by a victim. The man and the girl who occupied those two units could have been a pushover for a blackmailer.

"The police can't get a line on either one of them. They're referring to the man as Mr. X and the girl as Miss Y. Suppose Mr. X is a fairly well-known, affluent businessman and Miss Y is a week-end attraction, or perhaps someone who is scheduled to supplant Mrs. X as soon as a Reno divorce can be arranged. Suppose everything was all very hush-hush, and suppose Binney Denham found out about it. Binney drops in to pay his respects and make a little cash collection and gets a bullet in the back."

"Very interesting," Mason said. "How would Binney Denham have found out about it?"

Drake said, "Binney Denham had forty thousand bucks underneath the carpet on the floor of his apartment. You don't get donations like that in cash unless you have ways of finding out things."

"Interesting!" Mason said.

"You want to keep your nose clean on this thing," Drake warned.

"In what way?"

"You're representing somebody. I haven't asked you who it is, but I'm assuming that it could be Mr. X."

Mason said, "Don't waste your time assuming things, Paul."

"Well, if you're representing Mr. X," Drake said, "let's hope Mr. X didn't leave a back trail. This is the sort of thing that could be loaded with dynamite."

"I know," Mason said. "How about some of this coffee, Paul?"

"I'll try a little," Drake said.

Della Street poured the detective a cup of coffee. Drake tasted it and made a face.

"What's the matter?" Mason asked.

"Thermos coffee," Drake said. "I'll bet it was made around midnight."

"You're wrong," Della Street said. "I had it renewed a little after three this morning."

"Probably my stomach," Drake said apologetically. "I've got fuzz on my tongue and the inside of my stomach feels like a jar of sour library paste. Comes from spending too many nights living on coffee, hamburgers and bicarbonate of soda."

"Anybody hear the shot?" Mason asked.

"Too many," Drake said. "Some people think there was a shot about eight-fifteen; some others at eight forty-five; some at nine-thirty. Police may be able to tell more about the time of death after the autopsy.

"The trouble is this Staylonger joint is on the main highway and there's a little grade and a curve there right before you get to turn-in for the motel. Trucks slack up on the throttle when they come to this curve and grade, and quite a few of them backfire. People don't pay much attention to sounds like that. There are too many of them."

Drake finished the coffee. "I'm going down and get some ham and eggs. Want to go?"

Mason shook his head. "Sticking around a while, Paul."

"Jeepers!" Drake said. "Mr. X must be a millionaire."

"Just talking, or asking for information?" Mason asked.

"Just talking," Drake said and heaved himself out of the chair.

Twenty minutes after he had left, Elsa Griffin tapped on the door of Mason's private office, and when Della Street opened the door, slid into the room with a furtive air.

Mason said, "You look like the beautiful spy who has just vamped the gullible general out of the secret of our newest atomic weapon."

"I did a job," she said enthusiastically.

"Good!" Mason told her. "What happened?"

"When I got there everything had quieted down. There was a police car in the garage and apparently a couple of men were inside units fifteen and sixteen, probably going over everything for fingerprints."

"What did you do?"

"I drove in to unit twelve, parked my car, went in and turned on the lights. I waited for a little while, just to see if anyone was going to show up. I didn't want to be dusting the place for fingerprints in case they did."

"What happened?"

"The manager came over and knocked on the door. He was sizing me up pretty much—I guess he thought perhaps I had a wild streak under my quiet exterior."

"What did you do?"

"I put him right on that. I told him that I was a member of a sorority and that we'd been having a reunion, that I came up to town for that and we'd had a pretty late party, that I was going to have to grab a few hours' shut-eye and be on my way in order to get back to my job."

"Did he say anything?"

"Not about the murder. He said there'd been a little trouble, without saying what it was, and then he said that some woman had been in my motel and asked if it was all right, and I told him, 'Heavens, yes,' that she was one of the sorority members who was to meet me and I'd told her that if I wasn't there to go in, make herself at home. I said I'd left the door unlocked purposely."

"Did he get suspicious?"

"Not a bit. He said there'd been some trouble and he'd been trying to check back on anything that had happened that was out of the ordinary; that he'd remembered this woman and he'd just wondered if it was all right."

"Tell you about what time it was?" Mason asked.

"Well, he didn't know the hour exactly, but as nearly as I can figure she must have been in there while I was out chasing that blonde. I had to follow her for quite a ways before I dared to swing alongside."

"And it *was* the blonde who was driving?"

"That's right, it was Geraldine Corning."

"What about fingerprints?" Mason asked.

She said, "I got a flock of them. I'm afraid most of them are mine, but some of them probably aren't. I have twenty-five or so that are good enough to use. I've put numbers on each of the cards that have the lifted prints and then I have a master list in my notebook which tells where each number came from."

"Clean up the place when you left?" Mason asked.

"I took a washrag, used soap and gave everything a complete scrubbing, then I made a good job by polishing it with a dry towel."

Mason said, "You'd better leave your fingerprints on a card so I can have Drake's men check these lifted prints and eliminate yours. Let's hope that we've got some prints of that prowler. Do you have any idea who she might have been?"

"Not the least in the world. I just simply can't understand it. I don't know why in the world anyone should have been interested in the cabin *I* was occupying."

"It may have been just a mistake," Mason said.

"Mr. Mason, do you suppose that these . . . well, these blackmailers became suspicious when I showed up? Do you suppose they were keeping the place under surveillance? They'd know me if they saw me."

Mason said, "I'm not making any suppositions until I get more evidence. Go down to Drake's office, put your fingerprints on a card, leave the bunch of lifted fingerprints there, tell Paul Drake to have his experts sort out all of the latents that are yours and discard them, and bring any other fingerprints to me."

"Then what do I do?"

Mason said, "It would be highly advisable for you to keep out of the office today."

"Oh, but Mr. Bedford will need me. Today will be the day when—"

"Today will be the day when police are going to come

to the office and start asking questions," Mason said. "Don't be too surprised if they should have the manager of The Staylonger Motel with them."

"What would that be for?"

"To make an identification. It would complicate matters if he found you sitting at your secretarial desk and then identified you as the occupant of unit twelve."

"I'll say!" she exclaimed in dismay.

"Ring up Mr. Bedford. Explain matters to him," Mason said. "Don't tell him about having gone back to cabin twelve and taken the fingerprints. Just tell him that you've been up most of the night, that I think it would be highly inadvisable for you to go to the office. Tell Mr. Bedford that he'll probably have official visitors before noon, that if they simply ask him questions about the traveler's checks to tell them it's a business transaction and he cares to make no comment. If they start checking up on him and it appears that they're making an identification of him by his fingerprints as the man who drove that rented car or as the man who was in the motel, or if they have the manager of the motel along with them, who makes an identification, tell Mr. Bedford to keep absolutely mum.

"Have him put on a substitute secretary. Have her call my office and call the office of the Drake Detective Agency the minute anyone who seems to have any connections with the police calls at the office. Think you can do that?"

She looked for a moment in Mason's eyes and said, "Mr. Mason, don't misunderstand me. I'd do anything . . . anything in the world in order to insure the happiness or the safety of the man I'm working for."

"I'm satisfied you would," Mason said, "and that's what makes it dangerous."

"What do you mean?"

"In case he was being blackmailed," Mason said, "it might occur to the police that your devotion to your boss would be such that *you'd* take steps to get rid of the blackmailer."

"Oh, I wouldn't have done anything like *that!*" she exclaimed hastily.

"Perhaps you wouldn't," Mason told her, "but we have the police to deal with, you know."

"Mr. Mason," she ventured, "don't you think this Denham was killed by his partner? He mentioned a man, whom he called Delbert. This Delbert was the insistent one."

"Could be," Mason said.

"I'm almost certain it was."

Mason looked at her in swift appraisal. "Why?"

"Well, you see, I've always had an interest in crime and detective work. I read a lot of these magazines that publish true crime stories. It was because of an ad in a magazine that I took my detective course by mail."

Mason flashed a glance at Della Street. "Go on."

"Well, it always seems that when a gang of crooks gets a big haul, they don't like to divide. If there are three, and one of them gets killed, then the loot only has to be split two ways. If there are two, and one of the men gets killed, the survivor keeps it all."

"Wait a minute," Mason said. "You didn't read that in the magazines that feature true crime stories.

"That gambit you're talking about now is radio, motion pictures and television. Some of the fiction writers get ideas about a murderer cutting down the numbers who share in the loot. The comic strips play that idea up in a big way. Where did you read this story?" Mason asked. "In what magazine?"

"I don't know," she admitted. "Come to think of it, I have the impression that this story I referred to was in a comic strip.

"You see, I like detective works. I read the crime magazines and see the crime movies—I suppose you can say I'm a crime fan."

"The point is," Mason said, "the authorities aren't going to charge any accomplice. They're going to charge Stewart Bedford. That is, I'm afraid they are."

"I see. I was just thinking, Mr. Mason. If a smart lawyer should get on the job and plant some evidence that would point to Denham's accomplice, Delbert, as the murderer, that would take the heat off Mr. Bedford, wouldn't it?"

"Smart lawyers don't plant evidence," Mason said.

"Oh, I see. I guess I read too much about crime, but the subject simply fascinates me. Well, I'll be getting along, Mr. Mason."

"Do that," Mason told her. "Go on home and make arrangements to be ill so that you can't come to the office. Don't forget to stop in at Paul Drake's office and leave your fingerprints."

"I won't," she promised.

When the door had closed Mason looked at Della Street. "That girl has ideas."

"Doesn't she!"

"And," Mason went on, "if *she* should plant some evidence against this Delbert . . . well, if she has any ideas of planting evidence against anyone, she'd better be damned careful. A good police officer has a nose for planted evidence. He can smell it a mile."

Della Street said, "The worst of it is that if she *did* try to plant evidence and the authorities found it had been planted, they'd naturally think *you* were the one who had planted it."

"That's a chance a lawyer always has to take," Mason said. "Let's go eat, Della."

◼ 8 ◼

By THE TIME MASON AND DELLA STREET HAD RETURNED from breakfast, Sid Carson, Paul Drake's fingerprint expert, had finished with the lifted fingerprints that had been left him by Elsa Griffin and was in Mason's office, waiting to make a report.

"Nearly all of the prints," he said, "are those of Elsa Griffin, but there are four lifted latents here that aren't hers."

"Which are the four?" Mason asked.

"I have them in this envelope. Numbers fourteen, sixteen, nine, and twelve."

"Okay," Mason said, "I'll save them for future reference. The others are all Miss Griffin's?"

"That's right. She left a set of her fingerprints and we've matched them up. You can discard all of them except these four."

"Any ideas about these four?"

"Not much. They could have been left by some prior occupant of the motel. A little depends on climatic conditions and what sort of cleaning the place had, how long since it's been occupied and things of that sort. Moisture in the air has a great deal to do with the time a latent fingerprint will be preserved."

"How are these latents?" Mason asked. "Pretty good?"

"They're darn good. Very good indeed."

"Any notes about where they were found?"

"Yes, she did a good job. She lifted the prints, transferred them to cards, then wrote on the back of the cards where they were from. Two of these prints were from a mirror; two of them came from a glass knob on a closet door. She even made a little diagram of the knob, one of the sort of knobs that have a lot of facets so you can get hold of it and get a good grip for turning."

Mason nodded, said, "Thanks, Carson. I'll call on you again if we get any leads."

"Okay," Carson said and went out.

Mason contemplated the fingerprints under the cellophane tape.

"Well?" Della Street asked.

Mason said, "Della, I'm no fingerprint expert, but—" He adjusted a magnifying glass so as to get a clearer view.

"Well?" she asked.

"Hang it!" Mason said. "I've seen *this* fingerprint before."

"What do you mean, you've seen it before?"

"There's a peculiar effect here—" Mason's voice trailed away into silence.

Della Street came to look over his shoulder.

"Della!" Mason said. His voice was explosive.

She jumped at his tone. "What?"

"That card Bedford left with us, the card showing his wife and her fingerprints—get that card from the file, Della."

Della Street hurried to the filing case, came back with the card which Bedford had left with Mason, the card which the blackmailers had given him in order to show the authenticity of their information.

"Good heavens!" Della Street said. "Mrs. Bedford wouldn't have been there."

"How do you know?" Mason asked. "Remember what Bedford told us about getting the telephone call from Binney at his house while he was entertaining guests, that he wanted to talk in privacy, so he said he went up to his study and told the butler to hang up the phone as soon as he answered? Suppose Mrs. Bedford became suspicious. Suppose she sent the butler on an errand, telling him that she'd take over and hang up the phone. Suppose she listened in on the conversation and knew—"

"You mean . . . found out about—"

"Let's be realistic about this thing," Mason said. "When was this crime of defrauding the insurance company committed?"

"Several years ago, before her first marriage," Della Street said.

"Exactly," Mason told her. "Then she married, her husband committed suicide, she came into some money from insurance policies; then it was a couple of years before she married Bedford and a couple of years after the marriage before the blackmailers started to put the bite on Bedford.

"Yet, when the police went to Binney Denham's place, they found the floor carpeted with crisp new hundred dollar bills."

"You mean they'd been blackmailing her and—"

"Why wouldn't they?" Mason said. "Let's take a look at these fingerprints. If she knew Binney was starting to put the bite on her husband . . . a woman in that situation could become very, very desperate."

"But Mr. Bedford said they took such great precautions to see that they weren't followed. You remember what he told us about how the girl had him drive around and around and Binney followed in his car, and then Bedford picked the motel?"

"I know," Mason said, "but let's just take a look. I've seen this fingerprint before."

Mason took a magnifying glass, started examining the fingerprints on the card, then compared the two lifted fingerprints with the prints on the card.

He gave a low whistle.

"Struck pay dirt?" Della Street asked.

"Look here," Mason said.

"Heavens!" Della Street said, "I couldn't read a fingerprint in a year."

"You can read these two," Mason said. "For instance, look at this fingerprint on the card. Now compare it with the fingerprint here. See that tented arch? Count the number of lines to that first distinctive branching, then look up here at this place where the lines make a—"

"Good heavens!" Della Street said. "They're identical!"

Mason nodded.

"Then Mrs. Stewart G. Bedford was following—"

"Following whom?" Mason asked.

"Her husband and a blonde."

Mason shook his head. "Not with the precautions that were taken by the girl in the rented car. Moreover, if she'd been following her husband and the girl, she'd have known the units of the motel where they were staying and she would have gone in there."

"Then who was she following?"

"Perhaps," Mason said, "she was following Binney Denham."

"You mean Denham went to the motel to collect the money?"

Mason nodded. "Possibly."

"Then why would she have gone into Elsa Griffin's motel? How would she have known Elsa Griffin was there?"

"That," Mason told her, "remains to be seen. Get Paul Drake's office for me, Della. Let's put a shadow on Mrs. Stewart G. Bedford and see where she goes this morning."

"And then?" Della Street asked.

Mason gave the matter a moment of frowning concentration. "If I'm going to talk with her, Della. I'd better do it before the police start asking questions of her husband."

■ 9 ■

THE WOMAN WHO EASED THE LOW-SLUNG, FOREIGN-MADE sports car into the service station was as sleek and graceful as the car she was driving. She smiled at the attendant and said, "Fill it up, please," then, opening the car door, swung long legs out to the cement, holding her skirt tightly against her legs as she moved out from under the steering wheel.

She gave her skirt a quick shake, said to the attendant, "And we might as well check the oil, water, and battery."

She turned and confronted the tall man whose slim-waisted, broad-shouldered figure and granite hard features caused her to take a second look.

"Good morning, Mrs. Bedford. I'm Perry Mason."

"The lawyer?"

He nodded.

"Well, how do you do, Mr. Mason. I've heard of you, of course. My husband has spoken of you. You seem to know me, but I don't recall ever having met you."

"You haven't," Mason said. "You're meeting me now. Would you like to talk with me for a moment?"

Her eyes instantly became cold and wary. "About what?"

"About five minutes," Mason said, with a warning glance in the direction of the service station attendant who, while looking at the nozzle on the gasoline hose, nevertheless held his head at a fixed angle of attention.

For a moment she hesitated, then said, "Very well," and led the way back over toward an open space where

74

there were facilities for filling radiators and an air hose for tires.

"Now I'll ask you again. What do you wish to talk about, Mr. Mason?"

"About The Staylonger Motel and your visit there last night," Mason said.

The slate-gray eyes were just a little mocking. There was no sign to indicate that Mason's verbal shaft had scored.

"I wasn't visiting any motel last night, Mr. Mason, but I'll be glad to discuss the matter if you wish. The Staylonger Motel . . . it seems to me I've heard that name. Could you tell me where it is?"

"It's where you were last night," Mason said.

"I could become very annoyed with you for such insistence, Mr. Mason."

Mason took a card from his pocket, said, "This is the print of the ring finger on your right hand. It was found on the underside of the glass doorknob on the closet. Perhaps you'll remember that glass doorknob, Mrs. Bedford. It was rather ornamental—molded with facets that enable a person to get a good grip on the glass, but it certainly was a trap for fingerprints."

She regarded the lawyer thoughtfully. "And how do you know this is *my* fingerprint?"

"I've compared it."

"With what?"

"A police record."

She glanced away from him for a moment, then looked back at him.

"May I ask just what is your object, Mr. Mason? Is this some sort of a legal cat-and-mouse game? I am assuming that your reputation is such that you wouldn't be interested in the common, ordinary garden variety of blackmail."

Mason said, "The afternoon papers will announce the discovery of a murder at The Staylonger Motel. Police are naturally very much interested in anything out of the ordinary which happened there last night."

"And *your* interest?" she asked coolly.

"I happen to be representing a client, a client who prefers to remain anonymous for the time being."

"I see. And perhaps your client would like to involve me in the murder?"

"Perhaps."

"In which event I should talk with *my* lawyer instead of his—or hers."

"If you wish," Mason told her. "However, that probably wouldn't be the first conversation you'd have."

"With whom would I have the first conversation?"

"The police."

She said, "The attendant is finishing with my car. There's a hotel a few blocks down the street. It has a mezzanine floor, with a writing room and reasonable privacy. I'll drive there. You may follow me, if you wish."

"Very well," Mason told her. "However, please don't try any stunts with that powerful sports car of yours. You might be able to lose me in traffic, and that might turn out to be a rather expensive maneuver as far as you're concerned."

She stared at him levelly. "When you get to know me better, Mr. Mason—if you ever do—you'll learn that I don't resort to cheap, petty tricks. When I fight, I fight fair. When I give my word, I stay with it. Of course, I'm assuming you can move through traffic at a reasonable rate of speed without having a motorcycle officer take your car by the fender and lead it across the intersections."

With that she turned, walked over to sign the sales slip that the gasoline attendant handed her, then guided the low-slung car out into traffic.

Mason followed her until she swung into a parking lot. He parked his own car, entered the lobby of the hotel, took the elevator to the mezzanine and followed her to a writing table at which there were two chairs.

Everything about her appearance seemed to emphasize long lines. She was, Mason noticed, wearing long earrings; the carved ivory cigarette holder in which she fitted a cigarette was long and emphasized the length of the tapering fingers of her left hand which held the cigarette.

Mason seated himself in the chair beside her.

She looked at Mason and smiled.

"All the way up here I tried my damnedest to think up some way that I could keep you from questioning me," she said, "and I couldn't do any good. I don't know whether you're bluffing about my fingerprints and the police record, but I can't afford to call your bluff, in case it is a bluff. Now then, what do you want?"

"I want to know about the jewels and the insurance company."

She took a deep drag from the cigarette, exhaled thoughtfully, then abruptly gave in.

"All right," she said. "I was Ann Duncan in those days. I have always had a hatred of anything mediocre. I wanted to be distinctive. I wanted to stand out. I had to go to work. I was untrained. Nothing was open except the sheerest kind of office drudgery. I tried it for a while. I couldn't make it. My appearance was striking enough so that the men I worked for didn't want to settle just for the mediocre office services, which were all they were willing to pay for.

"About all I inherited from my mother's estate was some jewelry. It was valuable antique jewelry and it was insured for a considerable amount.

"I needed a front. I needed some clothes. I needed an opportunity to circulate around where I'd be noticed. I was willing to take a gamble. I decided that if I could meet the right kind of people in the right way, life might hold a brighter future—a future different from the drab prospect of filing letters all day and having a surreptitious dinner date with the man I was working for after he'd telephoned his wife the old stall about being detained at the office."

"So what did you do?"

"I went about it in a very clumsy, amateurish way. Instead of going to a reputable firm and having the jewelry appraised and making the right sort of a business transaction, I went to a pawnshop."

"And then?"

"I felt that if I could get some money as a loan, later on I could repay the loan and redeem the jewelry. I felt that I could parlay the money I received into something worthwhile."

"Go on."

"I was living with a penurious aunt, a nosy busybody. I shouldn't say that about her. She's dead now. But anyhow I had to account for the loss of the jewelry, so I tried to make it look like a burglary, and then I pawned the jewelry."

"And your aunt reported the burglary to the police?"

"That was where the rub came in."

"You'd intended she would?"

"Heavens, no!"

"Then what?"

"I wasn't prepared for all the embarrassing questions. The jewelry was insured and my aunt insisted that I had to file a claim. She got a blank, made it out, gave it to me to sign. The police investigated. The insurance company investigated. Then the insurance company paid me the amount for which the jewelry was insured. It was money I didn't want, but I had to take it in order to keep my aunt from finding out what I had done. I didn't spend it. I kept it intact.

"Then I told my aunt a whopping fib about going to visit some friends. I took the money I'd received from the pawnbroker, got myself some glad rags, and went to Phoenix, Arizona. I registered at one of the winter resort hotels where I felt I stood a chance of meeting the sort of people I was interested in."

"And what happened then?" Mason asked.

"Then," she said, "the police found the jewelry in the pawnshop. At first they thought they were just recovering stolen property. Then they got a description of the person who had pawned the jewels and began to put two and two together and . . . oh, it was hideous!"

"Go on," Mason told her. "What happened?"

"However," she said, "in the meantime I'd met a very estimable gentleman, an attorney at law, a widower. I don't know whether he would ever have been attracted to me if it hadn't been for the trouble I was in. He was a lawyer and I went to him for help. At first he was cold and skeptical, then when he heard my story he became sympathetic. He took an interest in me, helped straighten things out, saw that I met people.

"I had the most wonderful three months I'd ever had in my life. People liked me. I found that there is a great deal to the saying that clothes make the pirate.

"I met a man who fell for me hard. I didn't love him but he had money. He needed me. He was never sure of himself. He was always too damned cautious. I married him and tried to build his ego, to get him to face the world, to take a chance. I didn't do a very good job. He made a start, built up some degree of assurance, then got in a tight place, the old doubts came back and he killed himself. The pathetic part of it was that it turned out he had won the battle he was fighting. The news came an hour after he'd fired the shot that ended his life. I felt terrible. I should have been with him. I was at a beauty parlor at the time it happened. In a fit of despondency he pulled the trigger. He was like that. After his death his doctor told me he was what was known as a manic-depressive. The doctor said it was a typical case. He said I'd really prolonged his life by helping to give him stability. He said they had suicidal compulsions in their moments of deep depression and that sometimes the fits came on them suddenly.

"My husband left me quite a bit of property and there was considerable insurance. I was moving in the right set then. I met Stewart Bedford.

"Stewart Bedford fascinated me. He's twenty years older than I am. I know what that means. There isn't a great deal of difference between thirty-two and fifty-two. There's a lot of difference between forty-two and sixty-two, and there's an absolutely tragic difference between fifty-two and seventy-two. You can figure it out mathematically, and you can't get any decent answer, no matter how you go at it. Stewart Bedford saw me and wanted me. He wanted me in the same way an art collector would want a painting which appealed to him and on which he had set his heart.

"I agreed to marry him. I found out that he wanted to show me off to his friends, and his friends move in the highest social circles.

"That was something I hadn't bargained on, but I tried to live up to my end of the agreement.

"And then this thing came up."

"What thing?"

"My record."

"How did it come up?"

"Binney Denham."

"He blackmailed you?"

"Of course he blackmailed me. It was hideous. I couldn't afford to have it appear that the wife Stewart Bedford was so proud of had been arrested for defrauding an insurance company."

"Then what?"

"Binney Denham is one of the most deceptive personalities you ever met. I don't know what to do with the man. He pretends that he is working for someone who is obdurate and greedy. Actually, Binney is the whole show. There isn't anyone else except a few people whom

Binney hires to do his bidding, and they don't know what it's all about.

"A week ago I got tired of being bled white. I told Binney he could go to hell. I slapped his face. I told him that if he ever tried to get another cent out of me, I'd go to the police. And, believe me, I meant it. After all, I'm going to live my own life and not go skulking around in the corners and shadows because of Binney Denham."

"And did you tell your husband?" Mason asked.

"No. In order to understand this, Mr. Mason, you have to know a little more about backgrounds."

"What about them?"

"Before my husband married me he'd been having an affair with his secretary—a faithful, loyal girl named Elsa Griffin."

"He told you that?"

"Heavens, no!"

"How did you find out?"

"I sized up the situation before I committed myself. I wanted to make certain that it was all over."

"Was it?"

"Yes, as far as he was concerned."

"How about her?"

"She was going to have her heart broken anyway, win, lose or draw. I decided to go ahead and marry him."

"Did your husband know that you knew anything about this secretary?"

"Don't be silly. I played them close to my chest."

"So you'd been paying blackmail, and you got tired of it?" Mason said.

She nodded.

"And what did you decide to tell your husband about it?"

"Nothing, Mr. Mason. I felt that there was a good even-money gamble that Binney would leave me alone if he knew I was absolutely determined never to pay him another cent. After all, a blackmailer can't make any money publicizing what he knows."

"Nowadays he can," Mason said. "There are magazines which like to feature those things."

"I thought of that, but I told Binney Denham that if the thing ever became publicized I'd go all the way, that I'd tell about the blackmail I'd been paying to him and that I had enough evidence so I could convict him."

"And then what?"

She avoided his eyes for a moment and said, "I'm hoping that's all there is to it."

Mason shook his head.

"You mean, he . . . he went after Stewart?"

"What makes you ask that?"

"I . . . I don't know. There was a telephone call night before last. Stewart acted *very* strangely. He went up to take the call in his room. The butler was to hang up the phone after my husband picked up the receiver upstairs, but the butler was called away because of an emergency and the downstairs phone was off the hook; I happened to be going by and I saw the phone off the hook and could hear squawking noises. I picked up the telephone to hang it up and they stopped talking just as I hung up the telephone. Over the receiver I thought I heard that whining, apologetic voice of Binney Denham. I couldn't distinguish words, just the tone of voice. And then I made up my mind it was just my imagination. I thought of asking my husband about the call, then decided to do nothing."

Mason said, "I'm afraid you're in a jam, Mrs. Bedford."

"I've been in jams before," she said with cool calm. "Suppose you tell me what you're driving at."

"Very well, I will. You've had this secret hanging over your head. You paid out thousands of dollars in blackmail. Then all of a sudden you became bold and—"

"Let's say I became desperate."

"That," Mason said, "is what I'm getting at. For your

information, it was Binney Denham who was murdered last night at The Staylonger Motel down near the beach."

Again her eyes gleamed with an indefinable expression. Then her face was held rigidly expressionless.

"Do they know who did it?" she asked.

"Not yet."

"Any clues?"

Mason, looking her straight in the eyes, said. "The manager saw a woman down there last night at about the time the murder was being committed, a woman who came out of unit twelve. She had evidently been prowling. The description the manager gave fits you exactly."

She smiled. "I suppose lots of descriptions would apply to me. Descriptions are pretty generalized anyway."

Mason said, "There are certain distinctive mannerisms you have. The manager gave a pretty good description."

She shook her head.

"And," Mason said, "certain fingerprints that were lifted from cabin twelve were unmistakably yours."

"They couldn't be."

"They are. I just showed them to you."

"Do the police know that you have them?"

"No."

"I tell you I wasn't there, Mr. Mason."

Mason said nothing.

"You've done quite a bit of legal work for my husband?"

"Some."

"Isn't there some way of faking or forging fingerprints?"

"There may be. Fingerprint experts say there isn't."

"These prints you mentioned are in this cabin?"

"Not now. They were developed and lifted from the places they were found in the cabin."

"Then what happened?"

"The cabin was wiped free of all prints."

"Someone is lying to you, Mr. Mason. Those can't be my fingerprints. There's some mistake."

"Let's not have any misunderstanding," Mason said. "Didn't you follow Binney Denham down to that motel some time last night?"

"Mr. Mason, why on earth would I follow Binney Denham down to any motel?"

"Because your husband was at that motel paying twenty thousand dollars' blackmail to Binney Denham."

She tightened her lips. Her face was wooden.

"You didn't follow Binney down there, did you?"

"I'd rather be dead than have that slimy little blackmailer get his clutches on Stewart. Why I'd . . . I'd—"

Mason said, "That is exactly the reasoning the police will follow in trying to determine a motivation."

"A reason why I should murder Binney Denham?"

"Yes."

"I tell you I wasn't there! I was home last night waiting for Stewart and your information about him is erroneous. He never went near that motel. He was at some stuffy old directors' meeting and working on a deal so delicate he didn't dare to leave the room long enough to telephone me. You're sure Binney Denham is dead? There can't be any doubt about it?"

"No doubt whatever," Mason said.

She thought that over for a moment, then got to her feet. "I'd be a liar and a hypocrite, Mr. Mason, if I told you I was sorry. I'm not. However, his death is going to create a problem you're going to have to cope with.

"The police will start checking Binney's background. They'll find out he was a blackmailer. They'll try to get a list of his victims in order to find someone who had a compelling motive to kill him. As the lawyer who handles my husband's problems you're going to have to see the police learn nothing of Binney's hold on me. Stewart loves to take me out socially and . . . well, it's hard to explain. I suppose in a way it's the same feeling an owner has

84

when he has a prize-winning dog. He likes to enter him in dog shows and see him carry off the blue ribbons. It's supposed to make other dog owners jealous or envious. Stewart loves to give me clothes, jewels, servants, background and then invite his friends to come in and look me over. They regard him as a very lucky husband, and Stewart likes that."

"And underneath you resent it?" Mason asked.

She turned again and looked him full in the eyes. "Make no mistake, Mr. Perry Mason. I love it. And as Stewart's lawyer you're going to have to find some way of saving him from a ruinous scandal. You'll have to find *some* way to keep from having my past brought to light."

"What do you think I am—a magician?" Mason asked.

"My husband does," she said. "And we're prepared to pay you a fee based on that assumption—and for proving those fingerprints are forgeries and that I wasn't anywhere near that motel last night."

With that she turned and walked away with long, steady steps, terminating the interview with dignity, finality, and in a way which left her complete mistress of the situation.

■ 10 ■

PERRY MASON TURNED HIS CAR INTO THE PARKING LOT by his building. The attendant, who usually saluted him with a wave of the hand, made frantic signals as he drove by.

Mason braked his car to a stop. The attendant came running toward him. "A message for you, Mr. Mason."

Mason took the sheet of paper. On it had been scribbled: "Police are looking for you. Della."

Mason hesitated a moment, thinking things over, then parked the car in the stall which was reserved for him and walked into the foyer of the office building.

A tall man seemed to appear from nowhere in particular. "If you don't mind, Mason, I'll ride up with you."

"Well, well, Lieutenant Tragg of Homicide," Mason said. "Can I be of some help to you, Lieutenant?"

"That depends," Tragg said.

"On what?" Mason asked.

"We'll talk it over in your office, if you don't mind."

They rode up in silence. Mason led the way down the corridor past the entrance door of his office, went to the door marked "Private," unlocked and opened the door.

Della Street's voice sharp with apprehension, said, "Chief, the police are looking for . . . oh!" she exclaimed as her eyes focused on Lieutenant Tragg.

Tragg's voice was gravely courteous as he said, "Good morning, Miss Street," but there was a certain annoyance manifest as he went on, "And how did you know the police were looking for Mr. Mason?"

"I just heard it somewhere. There isn't supposed to be anything secret about it, is there?" Della Street asked demurely.

"Apparently not," Tragg said, seating himself comfortably in the client's chair and waiting for Mason to adjust himself behind the office desk.

"Cigarette?" Mason asked, extending a package to Tragg.

"Thanks," Tragg said, taking one.

Mason snapped his lighter and held the flame out to Tragg.

"Service!" the police lieutenant said.

"With a smile," Mason told him, lighting his own cigarette.

Lieutenant Tragg, almost as tall as the lawyer, was

typical of the modern police officer who is schooled in his profession and follows the work because he enjoys it, just as his associate, Sergeant Holcomb, who made no secret of his enmity for Perry Mason, typified the old school of hard-boiled, belligerent cop. Between Mason and Tragg there was a genuine mutual respect and a personal liking.

"Staylonger Motel," Lieutenant Tragg said, looking at Mason.

Mason raised his eyebrows.

"Mean anything to you?"

"Nice name," Mason said.

"Ever been there?"

Mason shook his head.

"Some client of yours been there?"

"I'm sure I couldn't say. I have quite a few clients, you know, and I presume some of them stay at motels rather frequently. It's quite convenient when you're traveling by auto. You can get at your baggage when you want it and—"

"Never mind the window dressing," Tragg said. "We had a murder at The Staylonger Motel last night."

"Indeed?" Mason said. "Who was murdered?"

"A man by the name of Binney Denham. Rather an interesting character, too, as it turns out."

"Client of mine?" Mason asked.

"I hope not."

"But I take it there's *some* connection," Mason told him.

"I wouldn't be too surprised."

"Want to tell me about it?"

"I'll tell you some of the things we know," Tragg said. "Yesterday afternoon a man who looked the executive type, with dark hair, iron gray at the temples, trim figure, well-tailored clothes, and an air of success, showed up at The Staylonger Motel with a woman who was quite a bit younger. The man could have been fifty. The woman, who was blonde and seductive, could have been twenty-five."

"Tut-tut-tut!" Mason said.

Tragg grinned. "Yeah! I know. Almost unique in the annals of motel history, isn't it? Well, here's the funny part. The man insisted on a double cabin; said they were going to be joined by another couple. However, after getting two units with a connecting door, the man apparently parked the blonde in unit sixteen and established his domicile in unit fifteen.

"The man was driving a rented car. They had drinks, went out, came back, and that evening the blonde drove away—alone.

"At around eleven last night the police received a call from an unknown woman. The woman said she wanted to report a homicide at unit sixteen in The Staylonger Motel, and then the woman hung up."

"Just like that?" Mason asked.

"Just like that," Tragg said. "Interesting, isn't it?"

"In what way?"

"Oh, I don't know," Tragg said. "But when you stop to look at it, it has a peculiar pattern. Why should a woman call up to report a homicide?"

"Because she had knowledge that she thought the police should have," Mason said promptly.

"Then why didn't she state her name and address?"

"Because she didn't want to become involved personally."

"It's surprising the way you parallel my thinking," Tragg said. "Only I carry my thinking a step farther."

"How come?"

"Usually a woman who wants to keep out of a thing of that sort simply doesn't bother to report. Usually a woman who reports, if she's acting in good faith, will give her name and address. But if that woman had been advised by a smart lawyer who had told her, 'It's your duty to report the homicide to the police, but there's no law that says you have to stay on the phone long enough to give your name and address—' Well, you know how it is, Mason. It starts me thinking."

"It seems to be habit you have," Mason said.

"I'm trying to cultivate it," Tragg told him.

"I take it there's something more?" Mason asked.

"Oh, lots more. We made a routine check down at The Staylonger Motel. We get lots of false steers on these things, you know. This time it happened to be correct. This character was lying there in the middle of the floor with a bullet hole in his back. The executive-type businessman and the curvaceous-type blonde and the rented car had completely disappeared.

"The blonde had driven away in the car. The man had gone through a barbed wire fence out the back way. He'd torn his clothes on the barbed wire. He evidently was in a hurry."

Mason nodded sympathetically. "Doesn't leave you much to work on, does it?"

"Oh, don't worry about a little thing like that," Tragg said. "We have *lots* to work on. You see we have the license number of the automobile. We traced it down. It was a rented automobile. We got hold of the automobile, and we've come up with some pretty good prints."

"I see," Mason said.

"Shortly after we phoned in the order to impound this automobile, we received a telephone call from the man who runs the car rental agency. He said that a woman came in to rent a car, inquired about cars that were available, wanted a car of a certain type, looked over the cars that he had, and then changed her mind. She had a slip of paper with license number on it. She seemed to be looking for some particular car."

"Did she say what car?" Mason asked.

"No, she didn't say."

Mason smiled. "The manager of the car rental agency may have a vivid imagination."

"Perhaps," Tragg said. "But the woman acted in a way that aroused the suspicions of the manager. He thought perhaps she might be trying to get hold of this particular car that had figured in a homicide. When she left, he followed her around the block. She got in a car that was driven by a man. The manager took down the license number of the automobile."

"Very clever," Mason said.

"The automobile was registered in the name of the Drake Detective Agency."

"You've talked with Drake?" Mason asked.

"Not yet," Tragg said. "I may talk with him later on. The Drake Detective Agency has offices here in the building on the same floor with you and does all of your work. You and Paul Drake are personal friends and close business associates."

"I see," Mason said, tapping ashes from the end of the cigarette.

"So I started making a few inquiries on my own," Tragg said. "Nothing particularly official, Mason. Just checking up."

"I see," Mason said.

"I notice that when Paul Drake is working on a particularly important case and stays up all night, he has hamburgers sent up from the lunch counter a couple of doors down the street. I probably shouldn't be telling you this, Mason, because it never pays for a magician to expose the manner in which he does his tricks. It has a tendency to destroy the effect.

"However, I dropped in to the lunch counter this morning, had a cup of coffee, chatted with the manager, told him I understood he'd been delivering quite a few hamburgers the night before, said I'd like to talk with the man who was on the night shift. Well, he'd gone home but hadn't gone to bed as yet, and the manager got him on the phone for me. I thought it would just be the same old seven and six of deliveries to Drake's office, but I hit unexpected pay dirt. I found that you and your secretary were up all night, and that you had hamburgers and coffee."

Mason said thoughtfully, "That's what comes of trying to get service. I should have gone down myself."

"Or sent Miss Street for them," Tragg said, smiling at Della Street.

"And so?" Mason said. "You put two and two together and made eighteen. Is that it?"

"I haven't put two and two together as yet," Tragg said. "I'm simply calling your attention to certain factors which I haven't tried to add up so far.

"Now, I'm going to tell you something, Mason. Binney Denham was a blackmailer. We haven't been able to get *all* the dope on him as yet. He kept his books in some sort of code. We haven't cracked that code. We do have fingerprints from that rented car. We have some cigarette stubs from the ash tray. We have a few other things we aren't talking about just yet.

"Now if you happen to have a client who was susceptible to blackmail, if Binney Denham happened to be bleeding that client white and the client decided to get out of it by just about the only way you can deal with a blackmailer of that type, the police would be as co-operative as is consistent with the circumstances—if we received a little co-operation in return.

"What we don't know is just where this curvaceous blonde entered into the picture. There are quite a few things we don't know. There are quite a few things we do know. There are quite few things we are finding out.

"Now, a good, smart lawyer who had a client in a jam of that sort might make a better deal with the police and perhaps with the D.A. by co-operating all the way along the line than by trying to hold out."

"Are you speaking for the D.A.?" Mason asked.

Tragg ground out his cigarette in the ash tray. "Now

there, of course, you've come to the weak point in my argument."

"Your district attorney is not particularly fond of the ground I walk on," Mason pointed out.

"I know," Tragg conceded.

"I think, under the circumstances," Mason said, "a smart lawyer would have to play them very close to his chest."

"Well, I thought I'd drop in,' Tragg said. "Just sort of a routine checkup. I take it you don't want to make any statement, Mason?"

Mason shook his head.

"Keep your own nose clean," Tragg warned. "There are people on the force who don't like you. I just thought I'd give you a friendly warning, that's all."

"Sergeant Holcomb going to be working on the case?" Mason asked.

"Sergeant Holcomb *is* working on the case."

"I see," Mason said.

Tragg got up, straightened his coat, reached for his hat, smiled at Della Street, and said, "At times you're rather obvious, Miss Street."

"I am?" Della Street asked.

Tragg nodded. "You keep looking at that private, unlisted telephone on the corner of Mason's desk. Doubtless you're planning to call Paul Drake as soon as I'm out of the door. I told you this was a *friendly* tip. For your information, I don't intend to stop in at Drake's office on the way out and I don't intend to talk with him *as yet*.

"I would like to be very certain that nothing happens to put your employer out of business as an attorney, because then he couldn't sign your pay checks, and personally it's a lot more fun for me to deal with brains than with the crooked type of criminal lawyer who has to get by by suborning perjury.

"I just thought I'd drop in for a social visit, that's all, and it might be a little easier for you to keep out of trouble if you knew that I'm going to have to report what I've found out down at the lunch counter about the consumption of sandwiches and coffee in the Mason office during the small hours of the morning.

"I don't suppose the persons who entered and signed the night register in the elevator would have been foolish enough to have signed their own names, but of course we'll be checking that and getting descriptions. I wouldn't be too surprised if the description of the man and the woman who went to your office last night didn't check with the description of the man and the woman who registered in units fifteen and sixteen at The Staylonger Motel. And, of course, we'll have a handwriting expert take a look at the man's signature on the register the elevator man keeps for after-hours visitors.

"Well, I'll be ambling along. I have a conference with my zealous assistant, Sergeant Holcomb. I'm not going to mention anything to him about having been here."

Tragg left the office.

"Hang it!" Mason said. "A man will think he's being smart and then overlook the perfectly obvious."

"Lieutenant Tragg?" Della Street asked.

"Tragg nothing!" Mason said. "I'm talking about myself. Having hamburgers sent up from that lunch counter is convenient for us and damned convenient for the police. We'll remember to keep out of *that* trap in the future."

"Thanks to Lieutenant Tragg," she said.

"Thanks to a very worthy adversary who is very shortly going to be raising hell with our client," Mason said.

■ 11 ■

MASON CAREFULLY CLOSED THE DOOR LEADING TO HIS private office, moved over close to Della Street, and lowered his voice. "You're going to have to take a coffee break, Della," he said.

"And then what?"

"Then while you're taking the coffee break, make certain that no one is in a position to see the number you're dialing. Call Stewart Bedford and tell him that under no circumstances is he to try to communicate with me, that I'll call him from time to time from a pay station; tell him that the police realize I'm interested in the case and may be watching my office."

Della Street nodded.

"Now," Mason said, "we're going to have to be very, very careful. Lieutenant Tragg knows that Paul Drake is working on the case. Tragg is a deadly combination of intelligence, ability, and persistence.

"They've got hold of that automobile from the drive-yourself agency and they've developed fingerprints. They don't have any way of picking up Stewart Bedford from those fingerprints because they don't know whose fingerprints they are, but if they ever get a line on Bedford they can then take his fingerprints and *prove* that he was in the automobile."

"What about Mrs. Bedford?" Della Street asked. "Aren't you obligated to tell Mr. Bedford about her?"

"Why?"

"You're representing him."

"As his attorney," Mason said, "I'm supposed to be looking out for his best interests."

"His wife is mixed in it. Shouldn't he know?"

"How is she mixed in it?"

"She was down there at the motel. She had all the motive in the world. Chief, you know as well as I do that she went down there because she thought Binney Denham was putting the bite on her husband and she didn't intend to stand for it. There was only one way she could have stopped it."

"You mean she killed him?"

"Why not?"

Mason pursed his lips.

"Well, why not?" Della Street insisted.

Mason said, "In a case of this kind we don't know what we're up against until all of the facts are in, and by that time it's frequently too late to protect our client. In this case I'm protecting my client."

"Just the one client?"

"Just the one client, Stewart G. Bedford."

"Then aren't you obligated to tell him about . . . about his wife?"

Mason shook his head. "I'm a lawyer. I have to take the responsibility of reaching certain decisions. Bedford is in love with his wife. It's quite probable that he's more in love with her than she is with him. Marriage for her may have been something of a business proposition. For him it represented a complete romantic investment in a new type of life."

"Well?" she asked.

"If I tell him about his wife's having been down there, about the fact that she may be suspect, Bedford will become heroic. He'll want to take all the blame in case he thinks there's any possibility she's guilty.

"I'm somewhat in the position of a physician who has to treat a patient. He doesn't tell the patient everything he knows. He prescribes treatment for the patient and does his best to see that the patient gets the right treatment."

Della Street thought that over for a moment, then said, "Will the police be able to locate Bedford today?"

"Probably," Mason said. "It's just a matter of time. Remember, Bedford is vulnerable on two or three fronts. For one thing, he bought a lot of traveler's checks, countersigned them and turned them over to the blackmailers. They cashed them. Somewhere along the line they've left a back trail that Tragg will pick up. Also remember that Bedford scribbled a note which he gave to the waiter at the cocktail lounge, asking him to call Elsa Griffin and give her the name of the motel. He didn't sign his name to the message, but after the newspapers begin to talk about the murder at The Staylonger Motel, the waiter will probably remember that that was the name of the motel he was to give Elsa Griffin over the telephone."

"Do you suppose the waiter saved the message?"

"He could have," Mason said. "There was twenty dollars in it for him, and that was bound to have registered in his mind. He could very well have saved the note.

"About all we can do is try to stall things along while Paul Drake gets information about Denham's background and see if we can locate that blonde."

"All right," Della Street said, "I'll take my coffee break and telephone Mr. Bedford."

"How are you feeling, Della?"

"As long as I can pour the coffee in, I can keep the eyes open."

"You'd better go home early this afternoon and try getting some sleep."

"How about you?"

"I'll be all right. I may break away this afternoon myself. Things are now where we have to wait for developments. I'm hoping Drake can come up with something before Tragg gets a line on our client. Get yourself some coffee and then go on home and turn in, Della. I'll phone you if anything comes up."

"I'll stick it out a while longer. I wish you'd get some rest and let *me* stay on the job and call *you*."

Mason looked at his watch. "Wait until noon, Della. If Drake hasn't turned up something by that time, we'll both check out. I'll leave word with Drake's office where they can call me."

"Okay," Della Street said. "I'll call Bedford right away."

■ **12** ■

MASON STOPPED IN AT PAUL DRAKE'S OFFICE.

"You don't look bad," Mason said to the detective.

"Why should I?"

"Up all night."

"We get used to it. *You* look like hell."

"*I'm* not accustomed to it. What are you finding out?"

"Not too much. The police are on the job and that makes things tough."

"This man Denham," Perry Mason said. "He had this blonde girl friend."

"So what?"

"I want her."

"Who doesn't? The police want her. The newspaper people want her."

"What's the description?" Mason asked.

"The description the police have is a girl about twenty-five to twenty-seven, five feet three, maybe a little on the hefty side, slim-waisted, plenty of hips, and lots of chest."

"What do they have from the rented car, Paul?"

"No one knows. The police keep that pretty much of a secret. They have *some* fingerprints."

"And from the units at the motel?"

"They have fingerprints there, too."

Mason said, "I'll give you a tip, Paul. The police are wise that you're working on the case."

"It would be a miracle if they weren't. You can't try to get information in a case of this sort without leaving a trail that the police can follow. I suppose that means they've connected me with you?"

Mason nodded.

"And you with your client?" Drake asked, watching Mason sharply.

"Not yet."

"Be careful. They will."

"It's just a matter of time," Mason conceded. "I want to find that blonde before they do."

"Then you'll have to give me some information that they haven't got," Drake said. "Otherwise, things being equal, there isn't a whisper of a chance, Perry. The police have the organization. They have the authority. They have all the police records. I have nothing."

"I can give you one tip," Mason said.

"What's that?"

"In this business names don't mean anything," Mason told him. "But initials do. My client tells me this girl gave the name of Geraldine Corning. She had a new overnight bag and suitcase with her initials stamped in gilt— *G.C.*"

"You don't think she gave her right name to this client of yours?"

"I doubt it," Mason said. "But I have a hunch her initials are probably the same. The last name won't mean much, but there aren't too many first names that begin with *G*. You might try Gloria or Grace, for a start."

"Blondes with first names of Gloria or Grace are a dime a dozen," Drake said. "The city's full of them."

"I know, but this was a girl who was hanging around with particular people."

"And you know what happens when you ask questions about girls who are hanging around with people like that?" Drake asked. "You run up against a wall of silence that is based on stark fear. You can open up any source of information and have things going good, and then you can casually mention, 'Do you know a girl by the name of Grace or Gloria Somebody-or-other who was playing around with this blackmailer Binney Denham?' Well, you know what happens. They clam up as though you'd pulled a zipper."

Mason thought that over. "I see your point, Paul. But a lot depends on this. We've simply *got* to get this girl located. She must have had a charge account some place that was paid by her sugar daddy or—"

"You know what would happen if we tried to get a line on all the blondes who have accounts that are paid by sugar daddies? We'd—"

"No, no, now wait a minute!" Mason said. "I'm just trying to narrow the thing down for you, Paul. She must have had an account at a beauty parlor. She must have had contacts, perhaps not with Binney Denham but perhaps with this Harry Elston who had the lock box with Binney. What can you find out about him?"

"Absolutely nothing," Drake said. "Elston visited the joint-tenancy lock box and faded from the picture. He's crawled into a hole and pulled the hole in after him."

"The police want him?"

"Very much."

Mason said, "Blackmailers and gamblers. Gamblers go to race tracks. Try covering the race tracks. See if you can get a line on this blonde. She had relatively new baggage. It may have been bought for this occasion.

"I'm going out to my apartment and get some shuteye. I'd like to have you stay on with this personally for another couple of hours if you can, Paul. Then you can turn it over to your operatives and get some sleep."

"Shucks! I'm good for another day and another night," Drake said.

Mason heaved himself out of his chair. "I'm not. Call me whenever you get a lead. I want to find that blonde and interview her before the police do, and I have an idea things are going to get pretty rugged this afternoon. I want to be able to think clearly when the going gets rough."

"Okay," Drake said. "I'll call you. But don't get to optimistic about that blonde. She's going to be hard to find, and in blackmailing circles the word will have gone out for everybody to clam up."

■ 13 ■

MASON TOOK A HOT SHOWER, CRAWLED INTO BED, AND sank instantly into restful oblivion only to be aroused, seconds later, it seemed to him, by the insistent ringing of the telephone.

He managed to get the receiver to his ear and muttered thickly into the telephone, "Hello!"

Paul Drake's voice, crisp and businesslike, said, "The fat's in the fire, Perry. Get going."

"What?" Mason asked.

"Police checking back on Denham's associates got on the trail of some traveler's checks. It seems a whole flock of traveler's checks were cashed. They bore the signatures of Stewart G. Bedford. Because of his prominence, the police were reluctant to start getting rough until they'd made a complete check.

"They got photographs of Bedford and took them out to Morrison Brems, the manager of The Staylonger Motel. Brems can't be certain, but he thinks from the photographs the police had that Bedford was the man who registered with the blonde.

"The police have—"

"Have they made an arrest?" Mason interposed.

"No."

"Brought him in for inquiry?"

"Not yet. They're going to his office to—"

Mason said, "I'm on my way."

Mason tumbled into his clothes, ran a comb through his hair, dashed out of the apartment, took the elevator down, jumped into his car and made time out to Bedford's office.

He was too late.

Sergeant Holcomb, a uniformed officer, and a plainclothes detective were in Bedford's office when Mason arrived. A rather paunchy man with a gold-toothed smile stood patiently in the background.

"Hello," Mason said. "What's all the trouble?"

Sergeant Holcomb grinned at him. "You're too late," he said.

"What's the matter, Bedford?" Mason asked.

"These people seem to think I've been out at some motel with a blonde. They're asking me questions about blackmail and murder and—"

"And we asked you nicely to let us take your fingerprints," Sergeant Holcomb said, "and you refused to even give us the time of day. Now then, Mason, are you going to advise your client to give us his fingerprints or not?"

"He doesn't have to give you a damn thing," Mason said. "If you want to get his fingerprints, arrest him and book him."

"We can do that too, you know."

"And run up against a suit for false arrest," Mason

said. "I don't know anyone I'd rather recover damages from than you."

Sergeant Holcomb turned to the paunchy man. "Is this the guy?"

"I could tell better if I saw him with his hat on."

Sergeant Holcomb walked over to the hat closet, returned with a hat, slapped it down on Bedford's head. "Now take a look."

The man studied Bedford. "It looks like him."

Sergeant Holcomb said to the man in plain clothes, "Look the place over."

The man took a leather packet from his pocket, took out some various colored powders, a camel's-hair brush and started brushing an ash tray which he had picked up.

"You can't do that," Mason said.

"Try and stop him," Holcomb invited. "Just *try* and stop him. I don't know anyone I'd rather hang one on than you. We're collecting evidence. Try and stop us."

Holcomb turned to Bedford. "Now then, you got twenty thousand dollars in traveler's checks. Why did you want them?"

"Don't answer," Mason said, "until they can treat you with the dignity and respect due a man in your position. Don't even give them the time of day."

"All those checks were cashed within a period of less than twelve hours," Sergeant Holcomb went on. "What was the idea?"

Bedford sat tight-lipped.

"Perhaps," Holcomb said, "you were paying blackmail to a ring that was pretty smart. They didn't want you to be able to make a payoff with marked or numbered bills, so they worked out that method so they could cash the checks themselves."

"And thereby left a perfect trail?" Mason asked sarcastically.

"Don't be silly," Holcomb said. "The way those checks were cashed you couldn't tie them in with Binney

Denham in a hundred years. We'd never even have known about it if it hadn't been for the murder."

The plain-clothes officer studied several latent finger-prints which he had examined with a magnifying glass. Abruptly he looked up at Sergeant Holcomb and nodded.

"What have you got?" Holcomb asked.

"A perfect little fingerprint. It matches with the little fingerprint on the—"

"Don't tell him," Sergeant Holcomb interrupted. "That's good enough for me. Get your things, Bedford. You're in custody."

"On what charge?" Mason asked.

"Suspicion of murder," Holcomb said.

Mason said, "You can make any investigation you want to, or you can make an arrest and charge him with murder, but you're not going to hold him on suspicion."

"Maybe I won't hold him," Holcomb said, "but I'll sure as hell take him in. Want to make a bet?"

"Either charge him, or I'll get a habeas corpus and get him out."

Holcomb's grin was triumphant. "Go ahead, Counselor, get your habeas corpus. By the time you get it, I'll have him booked and have his fingerprints. If you think you can get a suit for malicious arrest on the strength of the evidence we have now, you're a bigger boob than I think you are.

"Come on, Bedford. Do you want to pay for a taxi, or shall we call the wagon?"

Bedford looked at Mason.

"Pay for the taxi," Mason said, "and make absolutely no statements except in the presence of your attorney."

"Fair enough!" Sergeant Holcomb said. "I don't need more than an hour to make my case bulletproof, and if you can get a habeas corpus in that time, you're a wonder!"

Stewart G. Bedford drew himself up to his full height. "Gentlemen," he said, "I desire to make a statement."

"Hold it!" Mason said. "You're not making any statements yet."

Bedford looked at him with cold, resolute eyes. "Mason," he said, "I have retained you to advise me as to my legal rights. No one has to advise me as to my moral rights."

"I tell you to hold it!" Mason said irritably.

Sergeant Holcomb said hopefully to Bedford, "This is *your* office. If you want him out, just say the word and we'll put him out."

"I don't want him out," Bedford said. "I simply want to state to you gentlemen that I *did* go to The Staylonger Motel yesterday."

"Now, that's better!" Sergeant Holcomb said, pulling out a chair and sitting down. "Go right ahead."

"Bedford," Mason said, "you may *think* you're doing the right thing, but—"

Sergeant Holcomb said, "Throw him out, boys, if he tries to interrupt. Go ahead, Bedford; you've got this on your chest and you'll feel better when you get rid of it."

"I was being blackmailed by this character Binney Denham," Bedford said. "There is something in my past that I hoped never would come out. Somehow Denham found out about it."

"What was it?" Holcomb asked.

Mason tried to say something, then checked himself.

"A hit-and-run," Bedford said simply. "It was six years ago. I had a few drinks. It was a dark, rainy night. It really wasn't my fault and I was perfectly sober. This elderly woman in dark clothes was crossing the street. I didn't see her until I was right on her. I hit her a solid smash. I knew the minute I had hit her there was nothing anyone could do for her. It threw her to the pavement with terrific force."

"Where was this?" Sergeant Holcomb asked.

"Out on Figueroa Street, six years ago. The woman's

name was Sara Biggs. You can find out all about her in the accident records.

"As I say, I'd had a few drinks, I know very well what I can do and I can't do when I'm drinking. I never drive a car if I'm sufficiently under the influence of liquor to have it affect my driving in the slightest. This accident wasn't due in any way to the few cocktails I'd had, but I knew that I *did* have liquor on my breath. There was nothing that could be done for the woman. The street was, at the moment, free of traffic. I just kept on going.

"I made it a point to check up on the accident in the papers. The woman had been killed instantly. I tell you, gentlemen, it was her own fault. She was crossing the street on a dark, rainy night in between intersections. Heaven knows what she was trying to do! She was out there in the street and that's all. As I learned afterwards, she was an elderly woman. She was dressed entirely in black. I didn't know *all* of these things at the time. All I knew was that I had been drinking and had hit someone and that it had been her fault. However, I'd had enough liquor so I knew I'd be the goat if I'd stopped."

"Okay," Sergeant Holcomb said. "So you beat it. You made a hit-and-run. This guy Denham found out about it. Is that right?"

"That's right."

"What did he do?"

"He waited for some time before he put the bite on me," Bedford said. "Then he showed up with a demand that I—"

"When?" Holcomb interrupted.

"Three days ago," Bedford said.

"You hadn't know him before that?"

"That was the first time in my life I ever met the slimy little rascal. He had this apologetic manner. He told me that he hated to do it, but he needed money and . . . well, he told me to get twenty thousand dollars in traveler's checks, and that was all there'd be to it.

"Then he told me he had to keep me out of circulation while the checks were being cashed. That was when he showed up yesterday morning. He had a blonde woman with him who gave the name of Geraldine Corning. She had a car parked in front of the building. I don't know how they'd secured that parking space, but the car was right in front of the door. Miss Corning drove me around until we were certain we weren't being followed; then she told me to pick out a good-looking motel and drive in."

"*You* picked out the motel, or *she* did?" Sergeant Holcomb asked.

"I did."

"All right. What happened?"

"We saw the sign of The Staylonger Motel. I suggested that we go in there. It was all right with her. I was already paying blackmail on one charge and I didn't propose to have them catch me on some kind of frame-up with a woman. I told the manager, Mr. Brems—the gentleman standing over there who has just identified me—that I expected another couple to join us and therefore wanted a double unit. He said I could do better by waiting until the other couple showed up and letting them pay for the second unit. I told him I'd pay the entire price and take both units."

"Then what?"

"I put Miss Corning in one unit. I stayed in the other. The door was open between the units. I tried to keep rigidly to myself, but it became too boring. We played cards. We had a drink. We went out for a drive. We stopped in a tavern. We had a very fine afternoon meal. We returned and had another drink. That drink was drugged. I went to sleep. I don't know what happened after that."

"Okay," Sergeant Holcomb said, "you're doing so good. Why not tell us about the gun?"

"I *will* tell you about the gun," Bedford said. "I had never been blackmailed in my life. It made me furious to think of doing business on that kind of a basis. I . . . I had a gun in my study. I took that gun and put it in my brief case."

"Go on," Holcomb said.

"I tell you the last drink I had was drugged."

"What time was that?"

"Sometime in the afternoon."

"Three o'clock? Four o'clock?"

"Probably four. I can't give you the exact hour. It was still daylight."

"How do you know it was drugged?"

"I could tell. I have never been able to sleep during the day. However, after I took this drink I couldn't focus my eyes. I saw double. I tried to get up and couldn't. I fell back on the bed and went to sleep."

"This blonde babe drugged the drink?" Sergeant Holcomb asked.

"I rather think that someone else had entered the motel during our absence and drugged the bottle from which the liquor was poured," Bedford said. "Miss Corning seemed to feel the effects before I did. She was sitting in a chair and she went to sleep while I was still awake. In fact, as I remember it, she went to sleep right in the middle of a conversation."

"They sometimes put on an act like that," Holcomb said. "It keeps the sucker from becoming suspicious. She dopes the drink, then pretends she's sleepy first. It's an old gag."

"Could be," Bedford said. "I'm just telling you what I know."

"Okay," Sergeant Holcomb said. "How did it happen you used this gun? I take it the guy showed up and——"

"I *didn't* use the gun," Bedford said positively. "I had the gun in my brief case. When I awakened, which was sometime at night, the gun was gone."

"So what did you do?" Holcomb asked skeptically.

"I became panic-stricken when I found the body of Binney Denham in that other unit in the motel. I took my brief case and my hat and went out through the back. I crawled through the barbed wire fence—"

"You tore your clothes?" Holcomb asked.

"I tore the knee of my pants, yes."

"And then what did you do?"

"I walked across the lot to the road."

"And then what?"

"Then I managed to get a ride," Bedford said. "I think, gentlemen, that covers the situation."

"He was killed with your gun?" Sergeant Holcomb asked.

"How do I know?" Bedford said. "I have told you my story, gentlemen. I am not accustomed to having my word questioned. I am not going to submit myself to a lot of browbeating cross-questioning. I have told you the absolute truth."

"What did you do with the gun?" Sergeant Holcomb said. "Come on, Bedford, you've told us so much you might as well make a clean breast of it. After all, the guy was a blackmailer. He was putting the bite on you. There's a lot to be said on your side. You knew that if you started paying you were going to have to keep on paying. You took the only way out, so you may as well tell us what you did with the gun."

"I have told you the truth," Bedford said.

"Nuts!" Sergeant Holcomb observed. "Don't expect us to believe a cock-and-bull story like that. Why did you take the gun in the first place if you didn't intend to use it?"

"I tell you I don't know. I presume I thought I might intimidate the man by telling him I had paid once, but that I wouldn't pay again. I probably had a rather nebulous idea that if I showed him the gun and told him I'd kill him if he ever tried to shake me down again, it might help get me off the hook as far as future payments were concerned. Frankly, gentlemen, I don't know. I never did make any really definite plan. I acted on impulse, some feeling of—"

"Yeah, I know," Sergeant Holcomb said. "I know all about it. Come on through with the truth now. What did you do with the gun after the shooting? Tell us that and then you'll have got it all off your chest."

Bedford shook his head. "I have told you all I know. Someone took my gun out of my brief case while I was sleeping."

Holcomb looked at the plain-clothes officer, said to Bedford, "Okay. We'll go talk with the D.A. You pay for the cab."

Holcomb turned to Mason. "You and your habeas corpus," he said. "This is one case that backfired on you. How do you like your client now, wise guy?"

Mason said, "Don't be silly. If Bedford had been going to shoot Denham, why didn't he do it *before* he paid the twenty thousand and save himself that much money?"

Sergeant Holcomb frowned for a moment, then said, "Because he didn't have the opportunity before he paid. Anyhow, he's smart. It would be worth twenty grand to him to give you that talking point in front of a jury.

"It's your question, Mason, and the D.A. will let you try to answer it yourself in front of the jury. I'll be there listening.

"Come on, Bedford. You're going places where even Perry Mason can't get you out. That statement of yours gives us all *we* need.

"Call the cab. We leave Mason here."

◼ 14 ◼

Mason, bone tired, entered the offices of the Drake Detective Agency.

"Drake gone home?" he asked the girl at the switchboard.

She shook her head and pointed to the gate leading to a long, narrow corridor. "He's still in. I think he's resting. He's in room seven. There's a couch in there."

"I'll take a peek inside," Mason said. "If he's asleep I won't disturb him. What's cooking? Anything?"

"He has a lot of operatives out and some reports are coming in, but nothing important. He's trying to locate this blonde young woman you were so anxious to find. He's left word to be called if we get anything on her."

"Thanks," Mason said. "I'll tiptoe down. If he's sleeping I won't disturb him."

Mason walked on down the corridor past a veritable rabbit warren of small-sized offices, gently opened the door of number seven.

This was a small office with a table, two straight-backed chairs, and a couch. Paul Drake lay on his back on the couch, snoring gently.

Mason stood for a moment in the doorway, regarding the sleeping figure, then eased out and closed the door.

Just as the door latched shut, the phone on the table shrilled noisily. Mason hesitated a moment, then gently opened the door.

Paul Drake came up to a sitting position on the couch. His eyes were still heavy with sleep as he groped for the telephone, got the receiver to his ear, said, "Hello . . . yes

. . . What is it? . . ." He sleep-sodden eyes looked up, saw Mason, and the detective nodded drowsily.

Mason saw Drake's expression suddenly change. The man galvanized into wakefulness as though he had been hit in the face with a stream of cold water. "Wait a minute," he said. "What's that address? . . . Okay, what's the name? . . . Okay . . . I've got it. I've got it."

Drake scribbled rapidly on a pad of paper, then said into the telephone, "Hold everything! Keep watch on the place. If she goes out, shadow her. I'll be out there right away—fifteen or twenty minutes. . . . Okay, good-by."

Drake banged the telephone, said, "We've got her, Perry."

"Who?"

"This Geraldine Corning babe."

"You're sure?"

"Her name's Grace Compton. I have the address here. You had a correct hunch on the initials on the baggage."

"How'd you locate her, Paul?"

"I'll tell you after we get started," Drake said, "Come on. Let's go."

Drake ran his fingers through his hair, grabbed a hat, started down the narrow corridor with Mason pounding along at his heels.

"Your car or mine?" Mason asked in the elevator.

"Makes no difference," Drake told him.

"We'll take mine," Mason said. "You do the talking while I'm driving."

Mason and the detective hurried across the parking lot, jumped into Mason's car. Drake was talking by the time the car was in motion.

"The location of the car rental agency gave us something to work on," Drake said. "We started combing the classified ad directory for stores in the neighborhood handling baggage. I've had five operatives on the job covering every place they could think of. One of them struck pay dirt. A fellow remembered having sold baggage to a blonde who answered the description and putting the initials *G.C.* on it. The blonde paid with a check signed 'Grace Compton,' and the man remembered the bank. After that it was easy. She's living in an apartment house, and apparently she's in at the moment."

"That's for us," Mason said. "Good work, Paul."

"Of course, it *could* be a false lead. After all, we're just working on a description and slender clues. There are lots of blonde babes who buy baggage."

"I know," Mason said, "but I have a hunch this is it."

Drake said, "Turn to the left at the next corner, Perry."

Mason swung the car around the corner, then, at Drake's direction, turned back to the right after three blocks.

"Find a parking place in here some place," Drake said.

Mason eased the car into a vacant place at the curb. He and Drake got out and walked up to the front of a rather ostentatious apartment house.

A man sitting in a parked car near the entrance to the apartment house struck a match, lit a cigarette. Drake said, "That's my man. Want to talk with him?"

"Do we need to?"

"No. Striking the match and lighting the cigarette means that she's still in there. That's his signal to us."

Mason walked up to the directory, studied the names, and saw that Grace Compton had apartment two-thirty-one.

"How about this door, Paul?" Mason asked, indicating the locked outer door. "Do we sound the buzzer in her apartment, or can you—?"

"That's easy," Drake said, looking at the lock on the outer door. He took a key from his pocket, inserted it in the lock. The door swung open.

"Let's walk," Mason said.

The climbed the stairs to the second floor, walked

back down the corridor and paused before the door bearing the number two-thirty-one.

"It's your show from here on," Drake said. "Of course, your hunch may be right and it may be wrong. All we have is a description."

"We'll take a chance," Mason said.

He pressed the bell button. A long, two shorts and a long.

They heard the quick thud of steps on the inside, then the door swung open. A blonde in lounging pajamas said, "My God! You—" She stopped abruptly at the sight of the two men.

"Miss Compton?" Mason asked.

Her eyes instantly became cautious. "What is it?" she asked.

"We just wanted to talk with you," Mason said.

"Who are you?"

"This is Paul Drake, a detective."

She said, "You can't pull that line of stuff with me. I—"

"I'm Perry Mason, a lawyer."

"Okay, so what?"

Mason said, "Know anything about The Staylonger Motel, Miss Compton?"

"Yes," she said breathlessly, "I was there. I was there with one of the big-name motion picture stars. He didn't want the affair revealed. He just swept me off my feet. Now I'm suing him for support of my unborn child. How did you know?"

Mason said, "Were you there with Mr. Stewart G. Bedford yesterday?"

Her eyes narrowed. "All right, if this is a pinch, get it off your chest. If it isn't, get out of here."

"It's not a pinch. I'm trying to get information *before* the police do."

"So you brought a detective along with you?"

"Private."

"Oh, I see. And you want to know just what I did yesterday. How perfectly delightful! Would you like to come in and sit down? I suppose you expect me to buy you a drink and——"

"You knew Binney Denham?"

"Denham? Denham?" she said and slowly shook her head. "The name means nothing to me. Am I supposed to know him?"

"If you're the one I think you are," Mason said, "you and Stewart Bedford occupied units fifteen and sixteen in The Staylonger Motel yesterday."

"Why, Mr. Mason, how you talk?" she said. "I never go to a motel without a chaperon . . . never!"

"And," Mason went on, "Binney Denham was found sprawled out stone dead in the unit you had been occupying. A .38 revolver had sent a bullet through his——"

She stepped back, her face white, her eyes wide and round. Her lips opened as though she might be going to scream. She pressed her knuckles up against her lips, hard.

Mason nodded to Paul Drake, calmly pushed his way into the apartment, closing the door behind him. He moved over to a chair, sat down, lit a cigarette, and said, "Sit down, Paul," acting as though he might have owned the apartment.

The girl looked at him for several long seconds, terror in her eyes.

At length she asked, "Is this . . . is this on the up and up?"

"Ring up the police," Mason said. "They'll tell you."

"What do *I* want with the police?"

"It's probably the other way around at that," Mason told her. "They'll be here any minute. Want to tell us what happened?"

She moved over to a chair, eased down to sit on the extreme edge.

"Any time," Mason said.

114

"What's *your* interest in it, Mr. Mason?"

"I'm representing Stewart Bedford. Police seem to think he might have had something to do with the murder."

"Gosh!" she said in a hushed voice. "He could have at that!"

"What happened?" Mason asked.

She said, "It was a shakedown. I don't know the details. Binney has hired me on several occasions to do jobs for him."

"What sort of jobs?"

"Keep the sucker out of circulation until Binney has the cash all in hand. Then Binney gives me a signal and I turn him loose."

"Why keep him out of circulation?" Mason asked.

"So he won't change this mind at the last minute and so we can be certain he isn't working with any firm of private detectives."

"What do you do?"

"I keep their minds on other things."

"Such as what?"

"Am I supposed to draw diagrams?"

"What did you do with Bedford?"

"I kept his mind on other things . . . and it was a job. He's in love with his wife. I tried to get him interested, and I might as well have been an ice cube on the drainboard of the kitchen sink. Then after a while we really did get friendly, and— Don't make any mistake about it. That's all it was. Just a good, decent friendship. I like the guy.

"I made up my mind then and there that that was to be my last play in the sucker racket. When I saw the way he felt about his wife, the way he . . . well, I'm young yet. There's still a chance. Maybe some man will feel that way about me some day if he meets me in the right way. He's never going to feel that way about me the way things are now."

"So what did you do?"

"That," she said, "is where somebody gave us both a double cross."

"What happened?"

"I went out. I left a bottle of liquor on the table. Somebody must have doped the liquor. We came back and had a drink. I didn't even know I was drugged until I woke up sometime after dark. Bedford was still sleeping. I'd given him about twice as much whisky as I took. I felt his pulse. It was strong and regular, so I figured there hadn't been any harm done. I thought for a while it might have been knockout drops, and those can be dangerous. I guess this was one of the barbiturates. It didn't seem to hurt anything."

"And then what?"

She said, "I took a shower and got dressed and put on some other clothes. I knew that it wouldn't be very long. The banks had closed and Binney should be showing up any minute."

"And he did?"

"He did."

"What did he tell you?"

"Told me that everything was clear and we could leave."

"Then what happened?"

"Then I accused him of drugging the drink, and he denied it. I got a little hot under the collar. I thought he didn't trust me any more. I was mad anyway. I told him that the next time he had a deal he could just get some other girl to do the job for him. One thing led to another. I told him Bedford was asleep. We tried to wake him up. We couldn't wake him. He'd get up—to a sitting position—and then lurch back to the pillows. He was limber-legged.

"Okay, there wasn't anything I could do about it. He was just going to have to sleep it off. I was mad at Binney, but that wasn't putting any starch in Bedford's legs.

"I wasn't going to stick around there. He had money. He could get a cab and get home. I pinned a note on his sleeve, saying things were all right, that he could leave any time. Then I went out to my car."

"Where was Binney Denham?"

"Denham was in his car."

"Then what did you do?"

"I drove back and turned the car in at the rental agency the way I was supposed to. On a deal of that sort I'm not supposed to try and get anything back on the deposit. I just park the car in the lot with the keys in it, walk toward the office as though I'm going to check in, and then just keep on going. They find the car parked, with the keys in it. There's a fifty-buck deposit on the thing and only eleven or twelve dollars due. They wait a while to see if anyone's coming back for the credit and then, after a while, some clerk clears the records, puts the surplus in his pocket and that's all there is to it."

"Did you leave Binney behind?"

"No, he pulled out about the same time I did."

"Then he must have turned around and gone back."

"I guess so. Was his car there?"

Mason shook his head. "Apparently not. What kind of a car?"

"A nondescript Chevy," she said. "He wants a car that nobody can describe, a car that looks so much like all the other cars on the road nobody pays any attention to it."

"Was there any reason for him to have gone back?"

"Not that I know of. He had the money."

"Was there anything he wanted to see Bedford about?"

"Not that I know. He had the dough. What else would he have wanted?"

Mason frowned. "It must have been something. He went back to see Bedford for some reason. He couldn't have left something behind, could he—something incriminating?"

"Not Binney."

"Do you know what the shakedown was?"

"Binney never tells me."

"What name did you give?"

"Geraldine Corning. That's my professional name."

"Planning on taking a trip?" Mason asked, indicating the new baggage by the closet door.

"I could be."

"Make enough out of this sort of stuff to pay?"

She said bitterly, "If I made a hundred times as much, it wouldn't pay. What's a person's self-respect worth?"

"Then you can't help Bedford at all?" Mason asked.

"I can't help him, and I can't hurt him. He paid, and paid up like a gentleman. It was quite a shakedown this time—twenty thousand bucks. All in traveler's checks."

"What did you do with them?"

"I got him to sign them and I put them out in the glove compartment of the rented car. That was what we had agreed to do. Binney was hanging around there some place where he could see.

"We'd made arrangements so that we were sure we were safe. We knew we couldn't be followed. We just cruised around until we were dead certain of that. I doubled and twisted and Binney followed until we knew no one was tailing us. Then I let Bedford pick whatever motel he wanted. That gave him confidence, relaxed him.

"I locked him in so he couldn't get out, went to the phone booth, called Binney, told him where I was and told him the mark had signed the traveler's checks."

"Then what?"

"Then I left them in the glove compartment of the rented car. That was the procedure we'd agreed on. Binney took the checks out and got them cashed."

"Do you have any idea how he went about doing it?"

She shook her head. "Probably he has a stand-in with

a banker friend somewhere. I don't know. I don't think he put them into circulation as regular checks. He just handled the deal his own way."

"How about Binney? Did he have an accomplice?"

She shook her head.

"He referred to a man he called Delbert."

She laughed. "Binney was the smooth one! Suckers would get so infuriated at this fictitious Delbert they could kill him with their bare hands, but they always had a certain sympathy for Binney. He was always *so* sweet and *so* apologetic."

"You were his only partner?"

"Don't be silly! I wasn't a partner. I was a paid employee. Sometimes he'd give me a couple of hundred extra, but not often. Binney was a one-way street on money. Getting dough out of that little double-crosser was—"

"Yes, go on," Mason prompted as her voice died down.

She shook her head.

"He double-crossed you?"

"Go get lost, will you? Why should I sit here and blab all I know. Me and my big mouth!"

Mason tried another line of approach.

"So you made up your mind it was your last case?"

"After talking with Bedford I did."

"How did that happen? What did Bedford say to you?"

"Damned if I know. I guess he really didn't say anything. It was the way he felt about his wife, the way he'd look right past me. He was so much in love with his wife he couldn't see any other woman. I got to wondering how a woman would go about getting the respect of a man like that . . . hell! I don't know what happened. Just put it down that I got religion, if you want to put a price tag on everything."

Mason said, "We only have your word for it. It was a sweet opportunity for a double cross. You yourself admit you had decided to quit the racket. You could have told Binney you were quitting. Binney might not have liked that. You admit you and Binney were in there working with Bedford, trying to get him to wake up. You had undoubtedly gone through Bedford's brief case and knew what was in it. When the party got rough you could have pumped a shot into Binney's back, gone through him to the tune of twenty thousand dollars, and simply driven away."

She said, "That's your nasty legal mind. You lawyers do think of the damnedest things."

"Anything wrong with the idea?"

"Everything's wrong with it."

"Such as what?"

"I told you I was quitting. I told you I'd got religion. Would I get moral and decide to quit a racket and then plan on bumping a guy off to get twenty grand? That'd be a hell of a way to get religion!"

"Perhaps you had to kill him," Mason said, watching her with narrow eyes. "Binney may not have liked the idea of your getting religion. He may have had ideas of his own. The party may have got rough."

She said, "You're bound to make me the fall guy, win, lose, or draw, aren't you? You're a lawyer. Your client has money, social position, political prestige. I have nothing. You'll throw me to the wolves to save your client. I'm a damn fool even to talk with you."

Mason said, "If you killed him in self-defense, I feel certain Mr. Bedford would see that you—"

"Get lost," she interrupted.

Mason got to his feet. "I just wanted to get your story."

"You've had it."

"If anything happened and you *did* have to act in self-defense, it would strengthen your case if you reported the facts to the police. You should also know that any evidence of flight can be construed as an admission of guilt."

She said sarcastically, "You've probably got a lot of things on your mind, Mr. Mason. I've got a lot of things on *my* mind now. I'm not going to detain you any longer and I'm not going to let you detain me."

She got up and walked to the door.

The two men walked slowly back down the stairs. "Have your operative keep her shadowed, Paul," Mason said. "I have a hunch she's planning on making a break for it."

"Want to try and stop her if she does?"

"Gosh no! I only want to find out where she goes."

"That might be difficult."

"See that your operative has money," Mason said. "Let him get on the same plane that she takes. Go wherever she goes."

"Okay," Drake said. "You go get in the car. I'll talk with my operative."

Mason walked over to his car. Drake walked past the parked automobile, jerked his head slightly, then walked on around the corner.

The man got out of the parked automobile, walked to the corner, overtook Drake, had a few minutes' brief conversation, then turned back to the car.

Drake came over to Mason and said, "He'll let us know anything that happens and he'll follow her wherever she goes; only the guy doesn't have a passport."

"That's all right," Mason said. "She won't have one either. Your man has enough money to cover expenses?"

"He has now," Drake said.

"We have to be certain she doesn't know she's being shadowed, Paul."

"This man's good. You want her to run, Perry?"

Mason said, somewhat musingly, "I wish she didn't give that impression of sincerity, Paul. Sure I want her to run. I'm representing a client who is accused of murder. According to her own story this girl had every reason to kill Binney Denham. Now if she resorts to flight I can accuse her of being the killer, *unless* the police find more evidence against Bedford. Therefore, I want her to have lots of rope so she can hang herself . . . but somehow she bothers me. The story she tells arouses my sympathy."

"Don't start getting soft, Perry. She's a professional con woman. It's her business to make a sob-sister story sound reasonable. It's my guess she killed Denham. Don't shed any tears over her."

"I won't shed any tears," Mason said. "And if she dusts out of here in a hurry I've just about got a verdict of not guilty in the bag for Stewart G. Bedford."

■ 15 ■

MASON SAT IN THE ATTORNEY'S ROOM AT THE JAIL AND looked across at Bedford.

"I presume," he said, "you had that hit-and-run thing all figured out so you could save your wife's good name and were willing to sacrifice yourself in order to keep her from becoming involved."

Bedford nodded.

"Well, why the devil didn't you tell *me* what you were going to do?" Mason asked.

"I was afraid you'd disapprove."

"How did you get the details?" Mason asked.

"I took care of that all right," Bedford said. "As it happens, it was a case that I knew something about. This old woman was related to one of my employees. The doctors had decided she needed rather an expensive operation. My employee didn't approach me on it, but he *did* tell the whole story to Elsa Griffin. She relayed it to me. I told her to see that the man was able to get an advance which would cover the cost of the operation, and then told her to raise his wages in thirty days so that the raise would just about take care of payments on the advance. Two nights later the old woman started to cross the street, apparently in sort of a daze, and someone hit her and hit her hard. They never did find out who it was."

"Will your employee get suspicious?" Mason asked.

"I don't think so. The story was not told to me but to Elsa Griffin. Of course, that's one angle that I've got to take care of. Elsa will handle that for me."

"Well, you've stuck your neck in the noose now," Mason said.

"It's not so bad," Bedford told him. "As I understand it, a felony outlaws within three years, so they can't prosecute me on the hit-and-run charge because it's over three years ago. Don't you see, Mason? I simply *had* to have something that they could pin on me so there would be an excuse for me to be paying blackmail to Denham. Otherwise, the newspaper reporters would have started trying to find what it was that Denham had on me, and of course they'd have thought about my wife right away, started looking into her past, and then the whole ugly thing would have been out.

"In this way, I've covered my tracks in such a way that no one will ever think to investigate Mrs. Bedford."

"Let's hope so," Mason told him.

"Now look, Mason. I think I know who killed Denham."

"Who?"

"You remember that there was a woman prowling around the motel down there, a woman whose presence can't be accounted for.

"Now, I've got this thing figured out pretty well. Denham was a blackmailer. Someone decided that the only way out was to see that Denham was killed. The only way to kill him so that it wouldn't arouse suspicion and point directly to the person committing the murder was to wait until Denham was blackmailing someone else and then pull the job. In that way, it would be a perfect setup. It would look as though the other person had done the job."

"Go on," Mason said.

"So, as I figure it, this woman was either shadowing Denham or had some way of knowing when Denham was pulling a job. She knew that he was blackmailing me. She followed Denham down to the motel. When he got the payment from me, she killed him."

"With your gun?" Mason asked drily.

"No, no, now wait—I'm coming to that. I tell you I've got the whole thing all figured out."

"All right," Mason said. "How do you have it figured out?"

"Obviously she couldn't have followed Geraldine Corning and me down to the motel. In the first place, Geraldine took all sorts of precautions to keep from being followed, and in the second place, I was the one who picked the motel after she made up her mind that we weren't being followed. She said I could pick any motel I wanted, and I picked that one."

"Okay," Mason said. "You're making sense so far."

"All right. This woman knew, however, that Denham was getting ready to put the bite on another victim, so she started shadowing Denham. Denham drove down to the motel to pick up the money. She didn't have anything on him at that time. He went back and cashed the checks. That was where this woman *knew* that Denham was on another job.

"So when Denham came back to tell Geraldine that the coast was clear, Geraldine left and the woman had her chance. She had to be hiding down there in the motel. Naturally, she couldn't hide right on the grounds, so she tried the doors of the adjoining units. It just happened that Elsa had left the door of twelve unlocked because she didn't have anything valuable in there. The woman slipped into unit twelve and used it as her headquarters. Then she must have killed Denham with *her* gun.

"After that she cased the place and found that I was lying there asleep, apparently drugged. My brief case was on the floor. Naturally, she got to wondering who I was and how it happened I was asleep, and she went through the brief case. She saw the card giving my name and address in the brief case and she found my gun in there. What better than for her to take out the gun and conceal it where it would never be found. In that way I would be taking the rap for Denham's murder."

"Could be," Mason said noncommittally.

"Therefore, I want you to move heaven and earth to find that woman," Bedford said. "When we find her and get the *real* murder weapon, the ballistics experts can prove that it was the gun with which the murder was committed. Then we can find out what she did with my gun after the shooting.

"Can't you see the play, Mason? This woman prowler the manager saw in unit twelve is the key to the whole mystery.

"Now, I understand you sent Elsa back to the cabin to get fingerprints. Evidently our minds were working along the same lines. Elsa says she got some very good fingerprints of this woman, particularly a couple she got from a glass doorknob."

"Of course, a lot of the prints were Elsa's," Mason pointed out.

"I know. I know," Bedford said impatiently. "But some of them weren't. Elsa didn't even open that closet door. The two fingerprints on the knob simply *had* to be those of the woman.

"Now, this manager of the motel—whatever his name is—had a chance to talk with this woman. He saw her coming out of the motel, asked her what she was doing and all of that stuff. That makes him a valuable witness. I want you to have your men talk to him again and get the most minute description possible. Then you have these fingerprints to work on. Now damn it, Mason! Get busy on this thing and play it from that angle. It's a hunch I have."

"I see," Mason said.

Bedford said impatiently, "Mason, I've got money. I've got lots of money. The sky is the limit in this thing. You get all the detectives in the city if you need 'em, but you find that woman. She's the one we want."

"Suppose she did kill him with your gun?"

"She couldn't have. She shadowed Denham down there for one purpose, and only one purpose; she intended to kill him. She'd hardly intend to kill him with her bare hands."

Mason said, "Before we go all out on *that* theory, I'd like to be certain the murder wasn't committed with your gun. In order to prove that we need to have either the gun or some bullets that were fired from it. You don't know of any trees or stumps where you put up a target for practice, do you?"

"You mean so you can find some old bullets?"

"Yes."

"No. I don't think I ever fired the gun."

"How long have you had it?"

"Five or six years."

"You signed a firearms register when you bought it?"

"I can't remember. I guess I must have."

Mason said, "I have another lead. I want you to keep it confidential."

"What's that?"

"The blonde who was with you in the motel."

"What about her?"

"She had the opportunity and the motive," Mason pointed out. "She is the really logical suspect."

Bedford's face darkened. "Mason, what's the matter with you? That girl was a good kid. She probably had knocked around but she wasn't the type to commit a murder."

"How do you know?" Mason asked.

"Because I spent a day with her. She's a good kid. She was going to quit the racket."

"That makes her all the more suspect," Mason said. "Suppose she told Binney Denham she was going to quit and he started putting on pressure. That left her with only one out. Binney must have had enough on her to crack the whip if she tried to get free."

Bedford shook his head emphatically. "You're all wet, Mason. Get after this woman in number twelve."

"And," Mason went on, "we could convince a jury that the blonde would logically have taken the gun from your brief case and used it, whereas any woman who was shadowing Binney, intending to kill him, would have had her own gun."

"That's what I'm telling you."

"So then, if you try to play it your way," Mason went on, "and the murder weapon does turn out to have been your gun, you're hooked."

"You play it the way I'm telling you," Bedford instructed. "I have a hunch on this and I always play my hunches. After all, Mason, if I'm wrong it'll be my own funeral."

"You may mean that figuratively," Mason told him, getting up to go, "but that's one thing you've said that's *really* true."

■ **16** ■

MASON WAS YAWNING WITH WEARINESS AS HE FITTED A latchkey to the door of his private office and swung it open.

Della Street looked up from her secretarial desk, said, "Hello, Chief. How's it coming?"

"I thought I told you to go home and go to bed."

"I went home. I went to bed. I slept. I'm back and ready for another night session if necessary."

Mason shuddered. "Don't even think about it. One of those is enough to last me for quite a while."

"That's because you're under such a strain. You can't relax in-between times."

"Today," Mason told her, "there haven't been any in-between times."

"Paul Drake phoned while you were gone. He says he has something he thinks will prove interesting. He wants to come down and talk with you."

"Give him a ring," Mason said.

Della Street called Paul Drake, using the unlisted telephone, and not putting the call through the switchboard.

Mason tilted back in the swivel chair, closed his eyes, stretched his arms above his head and gave a prodigious yawn. "The trouble with a case of this sort," he said, "is that you have to keep one jump ahead of the police, and the police don't go to bed. They work in shifts."

Della Street nodded, heard Drake's tap on the panels of the door, and got up to open it for him.

"Hi, Paul," Mason said. "What's new?"

"You look all in," Drake told him.

"I had a hard day yesterday, and then things really started coming pretty fast last night. How are the police doing?"

"The police," Drake said, "are jubilant."

"How come?"

"They've found some bit of evidence that makes them feel good."

"What is it, Paul?"

"I can't find out, and neither can anyone else. They seem to think it's really something. However, that isn't what I wanted to see you about at the moment. I suppose you've heard that your client, Bedford, has made another statement."

Mason groaned. "I can't get back and forth fast enough to keep up with his statements. What's he said this time?"

"He told reporters he wants an *immediate* trial, and the district attorney says that if Bedford isn't bluffing, he'll give it to him, that there's a date on the calendar reserved for a case which has just been continued. Because Bedford is a businessman and insists that his name must be cleared and all that stuff, it looks as though the presiding judge might go along with them."

"Very nice," Mason said sarcastically. "Bedford never seems to think it's necessary to consult his lawyer before issuing these statements to the press.

"What about Harry Elston, Paul? Have you been able to get any line on him?"

"Not a thing, and the police haven't been able to," Drake said. "Elston opened that safe-deposit box about nine forty-five last night. He had a brief case with him, and, as I said, no one knows whether he put in or took out, but police are now inclined to think he took out and *then* put in."

"How come?"

"It was a joint lock box in both names. Now there isn't a thing in there in the name of Harry Elston, but the box is jammed full of papers belonging to Binney Denham.

They're papers that just aren't worth a hang, things that nobody would keep in a lock box."

"Some people keep strange things in lock boxes," Mason said.

"These are old letters, receipted statements, credit cards that have expired, automobile insurance that's expired, just a whole mess of junk that really isn't worth keeping, much less putting in a safe-deposit box."

Mason pursed his lips thoughtfully.

"The point is," Drake went on, "that the lock box is full—just so jam full you couldn't get another letter in it. The police feel that the idea of this was to keep them from thinking anything had been taken *out*. They're pretty well convinced the lock box was full of cash or negotiable securities, that Elston found out Denham was dead, cleaned out the box and put this stuff in it."

"How'd he find out Denham was dead?" Mason asked.

"Well, for a while the police were very much interested in the answer to that one. Now they're not concerned any more. They think that they have a dead open-and-shut case against Bedford. They think that any jury will convict him of first-degree murder. The D.A. says he hasn't decided whether he will ask for the death penalty as yet. He has stated that, while he will be ever mindful of the responsibilities of his office, he has never received any consideration from Bedford's counsel and sees no reason for extending any courtesies."

Mason grinned. "He wants to send my client to the gas chamber in order to get even with me. Is that it?"

"He didn't express it that way in so many words, but you don't have to look too far in between the lines to gather his thought."

"Nice guy!" Mason said. "Anything else, Paul?"

"Yes. This is what I really wanted to see you about. I got a telephone call just before I came in here. The operative who was shadowing Grace Compton only had time for a brief telephone call. He's at the airport. Our blonde friend is headed for Acapulco, Mexico. I guess she wants to do a little swimming. My operative is keeping her under surveillance. He has a seat on the same plane. He didn't have time to talk. He just gave me a flash."

"What did you tell him?"

"Told him to go to Acapulco."

"When are they leaving?"

"There's a plane for Mexico City leaving at eight-thirty."

Mason looked at his watch. "And she's down at the airport already?"

Drake nodded.

"What the devil is she doing waiting down there?"

"Darned if I know," Drake said.

"How has she disguised herself?" Mason asked.

"How did you know about the disguise?" Drake exclaimed. "I hadn't mentioned it."

"Figure it out for yourself, Paul. She knows that police have a pretty damn good description of her. She knows that they're looking for her. When the police are looking for someone, they're pretty apt to keep the airport under surveillance. Therefore, if Grace Compton was going to Acapulco, Mexico, the logical thing would be for her to stay in her apartment until the last minute, then dash out and make a run to get aboard the plane. Every minute that she's hanging around that airport makes it that much more dangerous for her. Therefore she must have resorted to some sort of disguise which she feels will be a complete protection."

"Well," Drake said, "you hit the nail right on the head that time, Perry. She's disguised so that no one's going to recognize her."

Mason raised his eyebrows. "How, Paul?"

Drake said, "I don't know the details. The only thing I know is that my man told me she was so disguised, that if he hadn't followed her and seen her go through the transformation, he wouldn't be able to recognize her. You see, he had time for a flash but no details. He says she's waiting to take the plane to Acapulco, and that's all I know."

"He'll call in again?" Mason asked.

"Whenever he gets a chance he phones in a report."

"He's one of your regular operatives?"

"Yes."

"Do you suppose he knows Della Street?"

"I think he does, Perry. He's been up and down in the elevator a thousand times."

Mason turned to Della Street. "Go on down to the airport, Della. Get a cab. Paul's operative will probably phone in before you get there. See if you can contact him. Describe him, Paul."

Drake said, "He's fifty-two. He used to have red hair. It's turning kind of a pink now and he's bald on top, but Della won't see that because he wears a gray hat with the brim pulled fairly well down. He's a slender man, about five foot seven, weight about a hundred and thirty-five pounds. He goes for gray, wears a gray suit, a gray tie, a gray hat. He has gray eyes, and he's the sort of guy you can look directly at and still not see."

"I'll find him," Della Street said.

"Not by looking for him," Drake said. "He's the most inconspicuous guy on earth."

"All right," Della said, laughing, "I'll be looking for the most inconspicuous guy on earth. What do I do after that, Chief?"

Mason said, "You get this girl spotted. Try to engage her in conversation. Don't be obvious about it. Let her make the first break if possible. Sit down beside her and start sobbing in a handkerchief. Be in trouble yourself. If she's frightened that may make her feel she has a bond in common with you."

"What am I going to be sobbing about?" Della Street asked.

Mason said, "Your boy friend was to have flown

down from San Francisco. He's stood you up. You're waiting, watching plane after plane."

"Okay," Della said. "I'm on my way."

"Got plenty of money for expenses?"

"I think so."

"Go to the safe and take out three hundred bucks," Mason said.

"Gosh! Am I supposed to go to Acapulco too?"

"I'm darned if I know," Mason told her. "If she gives you a tumble and starts confiding in you, stay with her as long as she's talking. If that means getting on a plane, get on a plane."

Della Street hurried to the emergency cash drawer in the safe, took out some money, pushed it down in her purse, grabbed her hat and coat, said, "On my way, Chief."

"Phone in if you get a chance," Mason said. "Use the unlisted telephone."

When she had gone, Mason turned to Paul Drake. "Now let's find out about this girl's apartment, Paul."

"What about it?"

"Did she give it up or simply close it and lock it?"

"Gosh! I don't know," Drake said.

"Find out, and when you find out let me know. If she's given up the apartment, and it's for rent, get a couple of good operatives whom you can trust, a man and woman. Have them pose as a married couple looking for an apartment. Pay a deposit to hold the place, or do anything necessary so they can get in there and dust for fingerprints."

"You want some of this girl's prints?"

Mason nodded.

"Why?"

"So I can show them to the police."

"The best way to get them," Drake said, "would be to give the police a tip on what's happening."

Mason shook his head.

"Why not?" Drake asked. "After all, they have her fingerprints. They have them from the car and from the motel and—"

"And they're building up a case against Stewart Bedford," Mason said. "They wouldn't do a thing to this girl now. They'd think she was a red herring I was drawing across the trail. For another thing I want the prints of someone else who must have been in that apartment. However, the main reason I don't want the police in on it is that I don't dare risk the legal status of what's happening."

"What's the legal status of what's happening?"

"A killer is resorting to flight," Mason said.

Drake frowned. "You got enough evidence to convict her of murder, Perry, even if you have evidence of flight?"

Mason said, "I don't want to *convict* her of murder, Paul. I want to acquit Stewart G. Bedford of murder. See what you can do about getting fingerprints and be sure to tell your man to watch out for Della Street. I have a feeling that we're beginning to get somewhere."

■ 17 ■

IT WAS SEVEN O'CLOCK WHEN DELLA STREET MADE HER report over the unlisted phone.

"I'm in a booth out here at the airport, Chief. I haven't been able to get to first base with her."

"Did you contact Drake's man?" Mason asked.

"Yes, that is, he contacted me. Paul certainly described him all right. I was looking all around for an inconspicuous man and not being able to find him, and then something kept rubbing against me, and it was the elbow of the man standing next to me at the newsstand. I moved away and then suddenly I looked at him and knew that was the man."

"And you picked out Grace Compton?" Mason asked.

"He did. She'd have fooled me."

"What's she done?" Mason asked.

"Well, she has on dark glasses, the biggest lensed, darkest dark glasses I've ever seen. Her hair is in strings. She's wearing a maternity outfit with—"

"A maternity outfit!" Mason exclaimed.

"That's right," Della Street said. "With a little padding and the proper kind of an outfit a girl with a good figure can do wonders."

"And you couldn't get anywhere with her?"

"Nowhere," Della Street said. "I've sobbed into my handkerchief. I've made every approach I could think of that wouldn't be recognized as an approach. I've got precisely nowhere."

"Anything else?" Mason asked.

"Yes. When she got slowly up and started for the restroom, I made a point of beating her to it. I knew where she was heading so I was in there first. I found out one reason why she's wearing those heavy dark glasses.

"That girl has had a beautiful beating. One eye is discolored so badly that the bruise would show below the edge of the dark glasses if she didn't keep it covered. She stood in front of a mirror and put flesh-colored grease paint on her cheek. I could see then that her mouth is swollen and—"

"And you're not getting anywhere?" Mason asked.

"Not with any build-up I can think of. No."

Mason said, "Go out and contact Drake's man, Della. Tell him that you'll take over the watching job while he calls me. Have him call me on this phone. Give him the unlisted number. Tell him to call at once. You keep your eye on the subject while he's doing it."

"Okay, I'll contact him right away, but I'd better not be seen talking to him. I'll scribble a note and slip it to him."

"That's fine," Mason said. "Be darn certain you're not caught at it. Remember, that's one bad thing about dark glasses. You can never tell where a person's eyes are looking."

"I'll handle it all right," she said, "and you can trust Drake's man. He can brush past you and pick up a note without anyone having the least idea of what's happened. He looks like a mild-mannered, shy, retiring, henpecked husband who's out for the first time without his wife, and is afraid of his own shadow."

"Okay," Mason said. "Get on the job. Now, Della, after this man telephones me and comes back out of the phone booth, grab a cab and come on back to the office."

"What a short-lived vacation!" she said. "I was thinking of a two-weeks' stay in Acapulco."

"You should have got her talking then. I can't pay out my client's money to have you sob your way down to Mexico unless you get results."

"My sobbing left her as cold and hard as a cement sidewalk," she said. "I should have tried a maternity outfit and the pregnancy approach. I can tell you one thing, Chief, that woman is scared stiff."

"She should be," Mason said. "Get Paul's man to phone, Della."

Some five minutes later Mason's unlisted phone rang. The lawyer picked up the receiver, said, "Hello," and a man's voice talking in a low, drab monotone, said, "This is Drake's man, Mr. Mason. You wanted me?"

"Yes. How did she work the disguise?"

"She came out of her apartment wearing a veil and heavy dark glasses. She got in a taxicab, went to the Siesta Arms Apartment House. She went inside. I couldn't see where she went, but I managed to butt my car into the rear end of the waiting taxi, got out and apologized profusely, got the guy in conversation, gave him five dollars to cover any damage that might have been sustained, which of course was jake with him because there wasn't any. He told me that he was waiting for a fare who had gone upstairs to pack up for her sister, that her sister was pregnant and was going to the airport to take a plane to San Francisco. This sister was to pick up the cab."

"Okay, then what happened?" Mason asked.

"Well, I waited there at the apartment house, right back of the cab. This woman didn't suspect a thing. When she came out, I would sure have been fooled if it wasn't for her shoes. She was wearing alligator skin shoes when she went in, and despite all the maternity disguise, she was wearing those same shoes when she came out. I let the cab driver take off, and I loafed along way, way behind, because I was pretty sure where they were going."

"They went to the airport?"

"That's right."

"And then what?"

"This woman got a tourist permit, bought a ticket to Acapulco, and checked the baggage. When she went down there she didn't have any more idea when the next plane was leaving than I did. She just sat down to wait for the next plane to Mexico City."

"She isn't suspicious?"

"Not a bit."

"Ride along on the same plane with her, just to make sure she doesn't try to disguise her appearance again. You'll be met in Mexico City by Paul Drake's correspondents there. You can work with them and they'll work with you. They know the ropes, speak the language, and have all the official pull they need. It will be better to handle it that way than for you to try and handle it alone."

"Okay, thanks."

"Now get this," Mason said. "This is important! You saw Paul Drake and me when we went up to call on Grace Compton?"

"That's right."

"You saw her when she came out?"

"Yes."

"She didn't come out and go anywhere between the time Drake and I left and the time she came out with the baggage and got the taxicab?"

"That's right."

"How much traffic was there in and out of that apartment building?"

"Quite a bit."

Mason said, "Some man went in. I'd like very much to spot him."

"Do you know what he looked like?"

"I haven't the faintest idea as yet," Mason said, "but I may have later. I'm wondering if you could recognize such a man if I dug him up. Could you?"

The expressionless voice, still in the same drab monotone, said, "Hell, no! I'm not a human adding machine. I was there to watch that blonde and see that she didn't give us the slip. Nobody told me to—"

"That's all right," Mason interrupted. "I was just trying to find out. That's all."

"If you'd told me, then I might have—"

"No, no, it's all right."

"Okay, anything else?"

"That's all," Mason said. "Have a good time."

For the first time there was expression in the man's voice. "Don't kid yourself, I won't!" he said.

When Della Street returned to the office, she found Perry Mason pacing the floor.

"What's the problem?" she asked.

Mason said, "I've got some cards. I've got to play them just right to be sure that each one of them takes a trick. I don't want to play into the hands of the prosecution so they can put trumps on my aces."

"Do they have that many trumps?" Della Sreet asked.

"In a criminal case," Mason said, "the prosecution has *all* the trumps."

Mason resumed his pacing of the floor, and had been pacing for some five minutes, when Drake's code knock sounded on the panel of the exit door.

Mason nodded to Della Street.

She opened the door. Drake came in and said, "Well, you had the right hunch, Perry. The babe's rent was up on the tenth. She told them there had been a change of plans because her sister expected to be confined in San Francisco and was having trouble. She said she had to leave for San Francisco almost immediately. She left money, for the cleaning charges and all that, and told the landlady how sorry she was."

"Wait a minute," Mason said. "Was this a face-to-face conversation or—?"

"No, she talked with the landlady on the telephone," Drake answered.

Mason said, "Some fellow gave her a working over. I'd sure like to find out who it was."

"Well," Drake said, "I put my operatives on the job and they tied up the apartment. They gave the landlady a fifty-dollar deposit, told her they wanted to stay in there and get the feel of the place for a while. She said to stay as long as they wanted.

"So they went all over the place for fingerprints and lifted everything they could find. Then they cleaned the place off so that no one could tell lifts had been made."

"How many lifts?" Mason asked.

Drake pulled an envelope out of his pocket. "They're all on these cards," he said. "Forty-eight of them."

Mason shuffled through the cards. "How are they identified, Paul?"

"Numbered lightly in pencil on the back."

"Pencil?"

"That's right. We ink the pencil in afterwards before we go to court. But just in case there are two or three prints you wouldn't want to use, you can change the numbers when they're written in pencil. In that way, when you get to court, your numbers are all in consecutive order. Otherwise, you might get into court and have prints from one to eight inclusive, then a gap of three or four prints, and then another set of consecutive numbers. That would be an invitation to opposing counsel to demand the missing fingerprints and raise hell generally."

"I see," Mason said.

"Well, that's it," Drake told him. "We've got our deposit up on the apartment. It won't be touched until the fifteenth. Now then, do you want the police to get a tip?"

"Not yet! Not yet!" Mason said.

"With that babe down in Acapulco, you may have trouble getting the evidence you want," Drake said.

Mason grinned. "I already have it, Paul."

Drake heaved himself up out of the chair. "Well, I hope you don't get another brain storm along about midnight tonight. See you tomorrow, Perry."

"Be seeing you," Mason said.

Della Street looked at Mason in puzzled perplexity. "You've got the expression of the cat that has just found the open jar of whipping cream," she said.

Mason said, "Go to the safe, Della. Get the fingerprints that Elsa Griffin got from that motel unit number twelve."

Della Street brought in the envelopes.

"Two sets," she said. "One of them the prints that were found to be those of Elsa Griffin, and the others are four that are prints of a stranger. These four are on numbered cards. The numbers are fourteen, sixteen, nine, and twelve respectively."

Mason nodded, busied himself with the cards Drake had handed him.

"All right, Della, make a note," he said.

"What is it?"

"Pencil number seven on Drake's list is being given an inked number fourteen. Number three on Drake's list given an inked number sixteen. Number nineteen on Drake's list given a number nine. Number thirty on Drake's list given the number twelve in ink. You got that?"

She nodded.

"All right," Mason said. "Take these cards and write the numbers in order on them—fourteen, sixteen, nine, and twelve. I want it in a woman's handwriting, and, while I wouldn't think of asking you to commit forgery, I'd certainly like to have the numbers as near a match for the numbers on these other cards as we can possibly make it."

"Why, Chief," Della Street said, "that's— Why those are the numbers of the significant lifted prints from unit twelve down there at the motel."

"Exactly," Mason said. "And as soon as you have these numbers copied on the cards, Della, you'll remember to produce them whenever I ask for latent prints on cards fourteen, sixteen, nine, and twelve."

"But, Chief, you can't do that!"

"Why not?"

"Why that's substituting evidence!"

"Evidence of what?"

"Why it's evidence of the person who was in that cottage. It's evidence that Mrs.—"

"Careful," Mason said. "No names."

"Well, it's evidence that that person was actually in that unit."

"How very interesting!" Mason said.

Della Street looked at him in startled consternation. "Chief, you can't do that! Don't you see what you're doing? You're just changing things all around. Why . . . Why—!"

"*What* am I doing?" Mason asked.

"Why you're numbering those cards fourteen, sixteen,

nine, and twelve and putting them in that envelope, and Elsa Griffin— Why she'll take the numbers on those cards, compare them with her notes and say that print number fourteen came from the glass doorknob and . . . well, in place of the person who was in there being there, it will mean that this blonde was in there instead."

Mason grinned. "And since the police have a whole flock of the blonde's fingerprints they'd have the devil of a time saying they didn't know who it was."

"But," Della Street protested, "then they would accuse Grace Compton of being the one who was in unit twelve when . . . when she wouldn't have been there at all."

"How do you know she wasn't there?" Mason asked.

"Well, her fingerprints weren't there."

Mason merely smiled.

"Chief, isn't . . . isn't there a law against that?"

"A law against what?"

"Destroying evidence."

"I haven't destroyed anything," Mason said.

"Well, switching things around. Isn't it against the law to show a witness a false—?"

"What's false about it?" Mason asked.

"It's a substitution. It's shuffling everything all around. It's—"

"There's nothing false about it," Mason said. "Each print is a true and correct fingerprint. I haven't altered the print any."

"But you've altered the numbers on the cards."

"Not at all," Mason said. "Drake told us that he put temporary pencil numbers on the cards so that it would be possible to ink in the numbers that we wanted."

Della Street said, "Well, you're practicing a deception on Elsa Griffin."

"I haven't said anything to Elsa Griffin."

"Well, you will if you show her these prints as being the ones that she took from that unit number twelve."

"If I don't *tell* her those were the prints that came

from unit number twelve, I wouldn't be practicing any deception. Furthermore, how the devil do we know that these prints are evidence?"

Della Street said, "Chief, *please* don't! You're getting way out on the end of a limb. In order to try and save Mrs. . . . well, you know who I mean if you don't want me to mention names. In order to save her, you're putting your neck in a noose and you're . . . you're *planting* evidence on that Compton girl."

Mason grinned. "Come on, Della, quit worrying about it. I'm the one that's taking the chances."

"I'll say you are."

"Get your hat," Mason told her. "I'll buy you a good steak dinner and then you can go home and get some sleep."

"What are *you* going to do?"

"Oh, I may as well go to bed myself. I think we're going to give Hamilton Burger a headache."

"But, Chief," Della said, "it's substituting evidence! Faking evidence! It's putting a false label on evidence! It's—"

"You forget," Mason said, "that we still have the original prints which were given us by Elsa Griffin. They still have the original numbers which she put on them. We've taken other prints and given them other numbers. That's our privilege. We can number those prints any way we want to. If by coincidence the numbers are the same, that's no crime. Come on. You're worrying too much."

JUDGE HARMON STROUSE LOOKED DOWN AT THE DEFENSE counsel table at Perry Mason, Mason's client, Stewart G. Bedford, seated beside him, and, immediately behind Bedford, a uniformed officer.

"The peremptory challenge is with the defense," Judge Strouse said.

"The defense passes," Mason said.

Judge Strouse glanced at Hamilton Burger, the barrel-chested, bull-necked district attorney whose vendetta with Perry Mason was well known.

"The prosecution is quite satisfied with the jury," Hamilton Burger snapped.

"Very well," Judge Strouse said. "The jurors will stand and be sworn to try the case."

Bedford leaned forward to whisper to Mason. "Well, now at least we'll know what they have against me," he said, "and what we have to fight. The evidence they presented before the grand jury was just barely sufficient to get an indictment, and that's all. They're purposely leaving me in the dark."

Mason nodded.

Hamilton Burger arose and said, "I am going to make a somewhat unprecedented move, Your Honor. This is an intelligent jury. It doesn't have to be told what I am going to try to do. I am waiving my opening statement. I will call as my first witness Thomas G. Farland."

Farland, being sworn, testified that he was a police officer, that on the sixth day of April he had been instructed to go to The Staylonger Motel, that he had met the manager there, a man named Morrison Brems, that he had exhibited his credentials, had stated that he wished to look in unit sixteen, that he had gone to unit sixteen and had there found a body lying on the floor. The body was that of a man who had apparently been shot, and the witness had promptly notified the Homicide Squad, which had in due time arrived with a deputy coroner, fingerprint experts, et cetera, that the witness had waited until the Homicide Squad arrived.

"Cross-examine!" Hamilton Burger snapped.

"How did you happen to go to the motel?" Mason asked.

"I was instructed."

"By whom?"

"By communications."

"In what way?"

"The call came over the radio."

"And what was said in the call?"

"Objected to as incompetent, irrelevant, and immaterial. Not proper cross-examination and hearsay," Hamilton Burger said.

Mason said, "The witness testified that he was 'instructed' to go to unit sixteen. Under the familiar rule that whenever a part of a conversation is brought out in direct examination the cross-examiner can show the entire conversation, I want to know what was said when the instructions were given to him."

"It's hearsay," Hamilton Burger said.

"It's a conversation," Mason said, smiling.

"The objection is overruled," Judge Strouse said. "The witness, having testified to part of the conversation, may relate it all on cross-examination."

"Well," Farland said, "it was just that I was to go to the motel, that's all."

"Anything said about what you might find there?"

"Yes."

"What?"

"A body."

"Anything said about how the announcer knew there was a body there?"

"He said it had been reported."

"Anything said about *how* it had been reported?"

"He said an anonymous telephone tip."

"Anything said about who gave the anonymous tip—whether it was a man's voice or a woman's voice?"

The witness hesitated.

"Yes or no?" Mason said.

"Yes," he said. "It was a woman's voice."

"Thank you," Mason said with exaggerated politeness. "That's all."

Hamilton Burger put a succession of routine witnesses on the stand, witnesses showing that the dead man had been identified as Binney Denham, that a .38 caliber bullet had fallen from the front of Denham's coat when the body was moved.

"Morrison Brems will be my next witness," Hamilton Burger said.

When Brems came forward and was sworn, Hamilton Burger nodded to Vincent Hadley, the assistant district attorney who sat on his left, and Hadley, a suave, polished courtroom strategist, examined the manager of the motel, bringing out the fact that on April sixth, sometime around eleven o'clock in the morning, the defendant, accompanied by a young woman, had stopped at his motel; that the defendant had told him he was to be joined by another couple from San Diego; that they wished two units; that the witness had suggested to the defendant it would be better to wait for the other couple to arrive and let them register, in which event they would be paying only for their half of the motel unit. However, the defendant had insisted on paying the whole charge and having immediate occupancy of the double.

"Under what name did the defendant register?" Vincent Hadley asked.

"Under the name of S. G. Wilfred."

"And wife?" Hadley asked.

"*And* wife."

"Then what happened?" Hadley asked.

"Well, I didn't pay too much attention to them after that. Of course, looking the situation over and the way it had been put up to me I thought—"

"Never mind what you thought," Hadley interrupted. "Just tell us what happened, what you observed, what you saw, what was said to you by the defendant, or by others in the presence of the defendant."

"Well, just where do you want me to begin?"

"Just answer the question. What happened next?"

"They were in there for a while, and then the girl—"

"Now, by the girl, are you referring to Mrs. Wilfred?"

"Well, of course she wasn't any Mrs. Wilfred."

"You don't *know* that," Hadley said. "She *registered* as Mrs. Wilfred, didn't she?"

"Well, the defendant here registered her as Mrs. Wilfred."

"All right. Call her Mrs. Wilfred then. What happened next?"

"Well, Mrs. Wilfred went out twice. The first time she went around to the outer door of unit fifteen and I thought she was going in that way, but—"

"Never mind what you thought. What did she *do?*"

"I know she locked him in, but I can't swear I saw the key turn in the lock, so I suppose you won't let me say a thing about that. Then after she'd done whatever it was she was doing, she went to the car and got out some baggage. She took that in to unit sixteen. Then a short time later she came out and went to the glove compartment of the car. I don't know how long she was there that time because I was called away and didn't get back for half an hour or so.

"Then quite a while later they both left the place, got in the car and drove away."

"Now just a minute," Hadley said. "Prior to the time

147

that you saw them drive away, had anyone else been near the car?"

"That I just can't swear to," Brems said.

"Then *don't* swear to it," Hadley said. "Just tell us what you know and what you saw."

"Well, I saw a beat-up sort of car parked down there by unit sixteen for a few minutes. I thought it was this other couple that had—"

"What did you *see?*"

"Well, I just saw this car parked there for a spell. After a while it drove away."

"Now the *car* didn't drive out. Someone must have driven it out."

"That's right."

"Do you know the person who was driving that car?"

"I didn't then. I do now."

"Who was it?"

"This here Mr. Denham—the man who was found dead."

"You saw his face?"

"Yes."

"Did he stop?"

"No, sir."

"He didn't stop when he drove his car out?"

"No, sir."

"Did he stop when he went in?"

"No, sir."

"All right. Now try to remember everything as you go along. What happened after that?"

"Well, of course I've got other things to do. I've got a whole motel to manage down there, and I can't just keep looking—"

"Just tell us what you saw, Mr. Brems. We don't expect you to tell us everything that happened. Only what *you saw.*"

"Well, the defendant and this girl—"

"You mean the one who had registered as Mrs. Wilfred?"

"Yes, that's the one."

"All right. What did they do?"

"They were out for quite a while. Then they came back in. I guess it was pretty late in the afternoon. I didn't look to get the exact time. They drove into the garage between the two units—"

"Now, just before that," Hadley interrupted. "While they were gone, did you have occasion to go down to the unit?"

"Well, yes, I did."

"What was the occasion?"

"I was checking up."

"Why?"

"Well . . . well, you see, when couples like that come in . . . well, we have three rates—our regular customer rate, our tourist rate, and our transient rate.

"Now, take a couple like this. We charge 'em about double the regular rates. Whenever they go out we check the units to see whether they're coming back or not.

"If they've left baggage, we look at it a bit if it's open. Sometimes if it isn't locked, we open it. Running a motel that way you have to cater to the temporary transients if you're going to stay in business, but you get high rates for doing it and usually a big turnover.

"Anyhow it isn't the sort of trade you like, and whenever the people go out, you go in and look around."

"And that's why you went in?"

"Yes, sir."

"And what did you do?"

"I tried the door of unit fifteen and it was locked. I tried the door of unit sixteen and *it* was locked."

"What did you do?"

"I opened the door with a passkey and went in."

"Which door?"

"Unit sixteen."

"What, if anything, did you find?"

"I found that the girl . . . that is, this Mrs. Wilfred . . . had a suitcase and a bag in unit sixteen and that the man had a brief case in unit fifteen."

"Did you look in the brief case?"

"I did."

"What did you see in it?"

"I saw a revolver."

"Did you look at the revolver?"

"Only in the brief case. I didn't want to touch it. I just saw it was a revolver and let it go at that, but I decided right then and there I'd better—"

"Never mind what you thought or what you decided. I'm asking you what you *did,* what you saw," Hadley said. "Now, let us get back to what happened after that."

"Yes, sir."

"Did you see the defendant again?"

"Yes, sir. He and this . . . this woman . . . this Mrs. Wilfred got back to the motel along late in the afternoon. They went inside and I didn't pay any more attention to them. I had some other things to do. Then I saw a car driving out somewhere around eight o'clock, I guess it was. Maybe a little after eight. I took a look at it and I saw it was this car the defendant had been driving, and this woman was in it. I didn't get a real good look at her, but somehow I didn't think anybody else was in that car with her."

"Had you heard anything unusual?"

"Personally, I didn't hear a thing. Some of the people in other parts of the motel did."

"Never mind that. I'm talking now about you personally. Did *you* hear anything unusual?"

"No, sir."

"And you so reported to the police when they questioned you?"

"That's right."

"When did you next have occasion to go to either unit fifteen or sixteen?"

"When this police officer came to me and said he wanted in."

"So what did you do then?"

"I got my passkey and went to the door of unit sixteen."

"Was the door locked?"

"No, sir. As a matter of fact, it wasn't."

"What happened?"

"I opened the door."

"And what did you see?"

"I saw the body of this man—the one they said was Binney Denham—lying sprawled there on the floor, with a pool of blood all around it."

"Did you look in unit fifteen?"

"Yes, sir."

"How did you get in there?"

"We went back out the door of unit sixteen and I tried the door of unit fifteen."

"Was it locked?"

"No, sir, it was unlocked."

"Was the defendant in there?"

"Not when we went in. He was gone."

"Was his brief case there?"

"No, sir."

"Did either the defendant or the woman who was registered by the defendant as his wife return to your motel later on?"

"No, sir."

"Did you subsequently accompany some of the authorities to the back of your lot?"

"Yes, sir. You could see his tracks going—"

"Now wait just a moment. I'm coming to that. What is in the back of your lot?"

"A barbed wire fence."

"What is the nature of the soil?"

"A soft, loam-type of soil when it's wet. It gets pretty hard in the summertime when the sun shines on it and it bakes dry. It's a regular California adobe."

"What was the condition of this soil on the night of April sixth?"

"Soft."

"Would it take the imprint of a man's foot?"

"Yes, sir, it sure would."

"Did you observe any such imprints when you took the authorities to the back of the lot?"

"Yes, sir."

"Are you acquainted with Lieutenant Tragg?"

"Yes, sir."

"Did you point out these tracks to Lieutenant Tragg?"

"I pointed out the route to him. *He* pointed out the tracks to *me*."

"And then what, if anything, did Lieutenant Tragg do?"

"Well, he went to the barbed wire fence right where the tracks showed somebody'd gone through the fence, and he found some threads. Some of the barbs on the barbed wire were pretty rusty and threads of cloth would stick easy."

"Now, from the time you saw Binney Denham, with his automobile which you have referred to as a rather beat-up car, near unit sixteen earlier in the day, did you see Mr. Denham again?"

"Not until I saw him lying there on the floor dead."

"Your motel is open to the public?"

"Sure. That's the idea of it."

"Mr. Denham could have come and gone without your seeing him?"

"Sure."

"You may cross-examine," Hadley said.

Mason said, "As far as you know, Denham could have gone into that unit sixteen right after the woman you have referred to as Mrs. Wilfred left, could he not?"

"Yes."

"Without your seeing him?"

"Yes."

"That's readily possible?"

"Sure it is. I look up when people drive in with automobiles and act like they're going to stop at the office, but I don't pay attention to people who come in and go direct to the cabins. I mean by that, if they drive right on by the office sign, I don't pay them any mind. I'm making a living renting units in a motel. I don't aim to pry into the lives of the people who rent those units."

"That's very commendable," Mason said. "Now, you rented other units in the motel during the day and evening, did you not?"

"Yes, sir."

"On the evening of April sixth and during the day of April seventh, did you assist the police in looking around for a gun?"

"Objected to as incompetent, irrelevant, and immaterial, not proper cross-examination," Hadley said, and then, getting to his feet, added, "If the Court please, we have asked this witness nothing of what he did on April seventh. We have only asked him about what took place on April sixth."

"I think, under the circumstances, the morning of April seventh would be too remote," Judge Strouse ruled. "The objection is sustained."

"Did you ever see that gun again?" Mason asked.

"I object to that as not proper cross-examination," Hadley said. "As far as the question is concerned, he may have seen it a week later. The direct examination of this witness was confined to April sixth."

"I'll sustain the objection," Judge Strouse ruled.

"Referring to the afternoon and evening of April sixth," Mason said, "did you notice anything else that was unusual?"

Brems shook his head. "No, sir."

Bedford leaned forward and whispered to Mason, "Pin him down. Make him tell about that prowler. Let's get a description. We've simply got to find who she is!"

"You noticed Binney Denham at the motel," Mason said.

"Yes, sir. That's right."

"And you knew that he wasn't registered in any unit?"

"Yes, sir."

"In other words, he was a stranger."

"Yes, sir. But you've got to remember, Mr. Mason, that I couldn't really tell for sure he wasn't in any unit. You see, this defendant here had taken two units and paid for them. He told me another couple from San Diego was coming up to join him. I had no way of knowing this here Denham wasn't the person he had had in mind."

"I understand," Mason said. "That accounts for the presence of Mr. Denham. Now, did you notice any *other* persons whom we might call unauthorized persons around the motel that day?"

"No, sir."

"Wasn't there someone in unit twelve?"

Brems thought for a minute, started to shake his head, then said, "Oh, wait a minute. Yes, I reported to the police—"

"Never mind what you reported to the police," Hadley interrupted. "Just listen to the questions and answer only the questions. Don't volunteer information."

"Well, there *was* a person I didn't place at the time, but it turned out to be all right later."

"Some person who was an unauthorized occupant of one of the motel units?"

"Objected to as calling for a conclusion of the witness and argumentative," Hadley said.

"This is cross-examination," Mason said.

"I think the word 'unauthorized' technically calls for the conclusion of the witness. However, I'm going to permit the question," Judge Strouse said. "The defense will be given the utmost latitude in the cross-examination of witnesses, particularly those witnesses whose direct examination covers persons who were present prior to the commission of this crime."

"Very well," Hadley said. "I'll withdraw the objection, Your Honor, just to keep the record straight. Answer the question, Mr. Brems."

"Well, I'll say this. A woman came out of unit twelve. She wasn't the woman who had rented the unit. I talked to her because I thought . . . well, I guess I'm not allowed to tell what I thought. But I talked to her."

"What did you talk to her about?" Mason asked.

"I questioned her."

"And what did she say?"

"Now there, Your Honor," Hadley said, "we are getting into something that is not only beyond the scope of cross-examination, but calls for hearsay evidence."

"The objection is sustained," Judge Strouse ruled.

"What did you ask her?" Mason asked.

"Same objection!" Hadley said.

"Same ruling."

Mason turned to Bedford and whispered, "You see, we're up against a whole series of technicalities there, Bedford. I can't question this witness about any conversation he had with her."

"But we've got to find out who she was. Keep after it. Don't let them run you up a blind alley, Mason. You're a resourceful lawyer. Fix your question so the judge has to let it in. We've *got* to know who she was."

"You say this woman who came out of unit twelve had not rented unit twelve?"

"That's right."

"And you stopped her?"

"Yes."

"And did you report this woman to the police?"

"Objected to. Not proper cross-examination. Incompetent, irrelevant, and immaterial," Hadley said.

"Sustained," Judge Strouse said.

"You have testified to a conversation you had with the police," Mason said.

"Well, of course, when things got coming to a head they wanted to know all about what had happened around the place. That was after they asked if they could look in unit sixteen to investigate a report they had had. I told them that they were welcome to go right ahead."

"All right," Mason said. "Now, as a part of that same conversation, did the police ask you if you had noticed any other prowlers during the afternoon or evening?"

"Objected to as incompetent, irrelevant, and immaterial, not proper cross-examination and hearsay," Hadley said.

Judge Strouse smiled. "Mr. Mason is now again invoking the rule that where part of a conversation has been brought out in direct examination, the entire conversation may be brought out on cross-examination. The witness may answer the question."

"Why, for the most part they kept asking me whether I'd heard any sound of a shot."

"I'm not talking about their primary interest," Mason said. "I'm asking if they inquired of you as to whether you had noticed any prowlers during the afternoon or evening."

"Yes, sir, they did."

"And did you then tell them, as a part of that conversation, about this woman whom you had seen in unit twelve?"

"Yes, sir."

"And what did you tell them?"

"Oh, Your Honor," Hadley said, "this is opening a door that is going to lead into matters which will confuse the issues. It has absolutely nothing to do with the case. We have no objection to Mr. Mason making Mr. Brems his own witness, if he wants to.

"He can then ask him any questions he wants, subject,

of course, to our objection that the evidence is incompetent, irrelevant, and immaterial."

"He doesn't have to make Mr. Brems his own witness," Judge Strouse ruled. "You have asked this witness on direct examination about a conversation he had with officers."

"Not a conversation. I simply asked him as to the effect of that conversation. Mr. Mason could have objected, if he had wanted to, on the ground that the question called for a conclusion of the witness."

"He didn't want to," Judge Strouse said, genially. "The legal effect is the same whether you ask the witness for his conclusion as to the conversation or whether you ask him to repeat the conversation word for word. The subject of the conversation came in on direct evidence. Mr. Mason can now have the entire conversation on cross-examination if he wants."

"But this isn't related to the subject that the police were interested in," Hadley objected. "It doesn't have anything to do with the crime."

"How do you know it doesn't?" Judge Strouse asked.

"Because we know what happened."

Judge Strouse said, "Mr. Mason may have *his* theory as to what happened. The Court is going to give the defendant the benefit of the widest latitude in all matters pertaining to cross-examination. The witness may answer to the question."

"Go on," Mason said. "What did you tell the officers about the woman in unit twelve?"

"I told them there'd been a prowler in the unit."

"Did you use the word 'prowler'?"

"I have the idea I did."

"And what else did you tell them?"

"I told them about talking with this woman."

"Did you tell them what the woman said?"

"Here again, Your Honor, I must object," Hadley said. "This is asking for hearsay evidence as to hearsay evidence. We are now getting into evidence of what some woman may have said to this witness and which conversation was in turn relayed to the officers. It is all very plainly hearsay."

"I will permit it on cross-examination," Judge Strouse ruled. "Answer the question."

"Yes, I said that this woman had told me she was a friend of the person who had rented that unit. She said she'd been told to go in and wait in case her friend wasn't at home."

"Can you describe that woman?" Mason asked.

"Objected to as incompetent, irrelevant, and immaterial. Not proper cross-examination," Hadley said.

"Sustained," Judge Strouse ruled.

Mason smiled. "Did you describe her to the officers at the time you had your conversation with them?"

"Yes, sir."

"How did you describe her to the officers?"

"Same objection," Hadley said.

Judge Strouse smiled. "The objection is overruled. It is now shown to be a part of the conversation which Mr. Mason is entitled to inquire into."

"I told the police this woman was maybe twenty-eight or thirty, that she was a brunette, she had darkish gray eyes, she was rather tall . . . I mean she was tall for a woman, with long legs. She had a way about her when she walked. Sort of like a queen. You could see—"

"Don't describe her," Hadley stormed at the witness. "Simply relate what you told the police."

"Yes, sir. That's what I'm telling—just what I told the police," Brems said, and then added gratuitously, "Of course, after that I found out it was all right."

"I ask that that last may go out as not being responsive to the question," Mason said, "as being a voluntary statement of the witness."

"It may go out," Judge Strouse ruled.

"That's all," Mason said.

Hadley, thoroughly angry, took the witness on redirect examination. "You told the police you thought this was a prowler?"

"Yes, sir."

"Subsequently you found out you were mistaken, didn't you?"

"Objected to," Mason said, "as leading and suggestive, not proper redirect examination. Incompetent, irrelevant, and immaterial."

"The objection is sustained," Judge Strouse said.

"But," shouted the exasperated assistant district attorney, "you subsequently *told* the police you *knew* it was all right, didn't you?"

"Objected to as not proper redirect examination," Mason said, "and as not being a part of the conversation that was testified to by the witness."

Judge Strouse hesitated, then looked down at the witness. *"When* did you tell them this?"

"The next day."

"The objection is sustained."

Hadley said, "You talked to the woman in unit twelve about it that same night, didn't you?"

"Objected to," Mason said, "as incompetent, irrelevant, and immaterial, calling for hearsay evidence, a conversation had without the presence or hearing of the defendant, not proper redirect examination."

"The objection is sustained," Judge Strouse ruled.

Hadley sat down in the chair, held a whispered conference with Hamilton Burger. The two men engaged in a vehement whispered argument; then Hadley tried another tack.

"Did you, the same night, as a part of that same conversation, state to the police that after you had talked with the woman you were satisfied she was all right and was telling the truth?"

"Yes, sir," the witness said.

"That's all," Hadley announced triumphantly.

"Just a moment," Mason said as Brems started to leave the stand. "One more question on re-cross-examination. Didn't you also at the same time and as a part of the same conversation describe the woman to the police as a prowler?"

"I believe I did. Yes, sir, at *that* time."

"That was the word you used—'a prowler'?"

"Yes, sir."

Mason smiled across at Hadley. "That's all my re-cross-examination," he said.

"That's all," Hadley said sullenly.

"Call your next witness," Judge Strouse observed.

Hadley called the manager of the drive-yourself car agency. He testified to the circumstances surrounding the renting of the car, the return of the car, the fact that the person returning it had not sought to cash in on the credit due on the deposit.

"No questions," Mason said.

Another employee of the drive-yourself agency testified to having seen the car driven onto the agency parking lot around ten o'clock on the evening of April sixth. The car was, he said, driven by a young woman, who got out of the car and started toward the office. He did not pay any attention to her after that.

"Cross-examine," Hadley said.

"Can you describe this woman?" Mason asked.

"She was a good-looking woman."

"Can you describe her any better than that?" Mason asked, as some of the jurors smiled broadly.

"Sure. She was in her twenties somewhere. She had ... she was stacked!"

"What's that?" Judge Strouse asked.

"She had a good figure," the witness amended hastily.

"Did you see her hair?"

"She was blonde."

"Now then," Mason asked, "I want to ask you a question, and I want you to think carefully before you answer it. Did you, at any time, see any baggage being taken out of the car after she parked it in the lot?"

The man then shook his head. "No, sir, she didn't take out a thing except herself."

"You're certain?"

"I'm certain."

"You saw her get out of the car?"

"I'll say I did."

There was a ripple of laughter in the courtroom.

"That's all," Mason announced.

"No further questions," Hadley said.

Hadley called a fingerprint expert, who testified to examining units fifteen and sixteen of The Staylonger Motel for fingerprints on the night of April sixth and the early morning of April seventh. He produced several latent prints which he had developed and which he classified as being "significant."

"And why do you class these as being significant?" Hadley asked.

"Because," the witness said, "I was able to develop matching fingerprints in the automobile concerning which the witness has just testified."

Hadley's questions brought out that the witness had examined the rented automobile, had processed it for fingerprints, and had secured a number of prints matching those in units fifteen and sixteen of the motel where the body had been found, that *some* of these matching fingerprints were, beyond question, those of the defendant, Stewart G. Bedford.

"Cross-examine," Hadley announced.

"Who left the other '*matching*' prints that you found?" Mason asked the witness.

"I assume that they were made by the blonde young woman who drove the car back to the agency and—"

"You don't *know?*"

"No, sir, I do not. I do know that I secured and developed certain latent fingerprints in units fifteen and sixteen of the motel, that I secured certain latent prints from the automobile which has previously been described as having license number CXY 221, and that those prints in each instance were made by the same fingers that made the prints of Stewart G. Bedford on the police registration card when he was booked at police headquarters."

"And you found the prints which you have assumed were those left by the blonde young woman in both units fifteen and sixteen?"

"Yes, sir."

"Where?"

"In various places—on mirrors, on drinking glasses, on a doorknob."

"And those same fingerprints were on the automobile?"

"Yes, sir."

"In other words," Mason said, "as far as your own observations are concerned, those *other* fingerprints could have been left by the murderer of Binney Denham?"

"That's objected to," Hadley said. "It's argumentative. It calls for a conclusion."

"He's an expert witness," Mason said. "I'm asking him for his conclusion. I'm limiting the question as far as his own observations are concerned."

Judge Strouse hesitated, said, "I'm going to permit the witness to answer the question."

The expert said, "As far as *I* know or as far as my observations are concerned, either one of them could have been the murderer."

"Or the murder *could* have been committed by someone else?" Mason asked.

"That's right."

"Thank you," Mason told him. "That's all."

Hamilton Burger indicated that he planned to examine the next witness.

"Call Richard Judson," he said.

The bailiff called Richard Judson to the stand. Judson,

an erect man with good shoulders, slim waist, a deep voice, and cold blue eyes which regarded the world with an air of a banker appraising a real estate loan, proved to be a police officer who had gone out to the Bedford residence on the tenth of April.

"And what did you do at the Bedford residence?" Hamilton Burger asked.

"I looked around."

"Where?"

"Well, I looked around the grounds and the garage."

"Did you have a search warrant?"

"Yes, sir."

"Did you serve the search warrant on anyone?"

"There was no one home; no one was there to serve the warrant on."

"Where did you look first?"

"In the garage."

"Where in the garage?"

"All over the garage."

"Can you tell us a little more about the type of search you made?"

"Well, there was a car in the garage. We looked over that pretty well. There were some tires. We looked around them, some old inner tubes—"

"Now, you say 'we.' Who was with you?"

"My partner."

"A police officer?"

"Yes."

"Where else did you look?"

"We looked every place in the garage. We looked up in the rafters, where there were some old boxes. We made a good job of searching the place."

"And then," Hamilton Burger asked, "what did you do?"

"There was a drain in the center of the garage floor— a perforated drain so that the garage floor could be washed off with a hose. There was a perforated plate which covered the drain. We unscrewed this plate, and looked down inside."

"And what did you find?"

"We found a gun."

"What do you mean, a gun?"

"I mean a .38 caliber Colt revolver."

"Do you have the number of that gun?"

"I made a note of it, yes, sir."

"That was a memorandum you made at the time?"

"Yes, sir."

"That was made by you?"

"Yes, sir."

"Do you have it with you?"

"Yes, sir."

"What do your notes show?"

The witness opened his notebook. "The gun was blued steel .38 caliber Colt revolver. It had five loaded cartridges in the cylinder and one empty, or exploded, cartridge case. The manufacturer's number was 740818."

"What did you do with that revolver?"

"I turned it over to Arthur Merriam."

"Who is he?"

"He is one of the police experts on firearms and ballistics."

"You may cross-examine," Hamilton Burger said to Perry Mason.

"Now as I understand it, you had a search warrant, Mr. Judson?" Mason asked.

"Yes, sir."

"And what premises were included in the search warrant?"

"The house the grounds, the garage."

"There was no one home on whom you could serve this search warrant?"

"No, sir, not at the time we made the search."

"When was the search warrant dated?"

"I believe the eighth."

"You got it on the morning of the eighth?"

"I don't know the exact time of day."

"It was in the morning?"

"I think perhaps it was."

"And after you got the search warrant what did you do?"

"Put it in my pocket."

"And what did you do after that?"

"I was working on the case."

"What did you do while you were, as you say, working on the case and after putting the search warrant in your pocket?"

"I drove around looking things over."

"Actually, you drove out to the Bedford house, didn't you?"

"Well, we were working on the case, looking things over. We cruised around that vicinity."

"And then you *parked* your car, didn't you?"

"Yes, sir."

"From a spot where you could see the garage?"

"Well, yes."

"And you waited all that day, did you not?"

"The rest of the day, yes, sir."

"And the next day you were back on the job again?"

"Yes, sir."

"Same place?"

"Yes, sir."

"And you waited all that day?"

"Yes, sir."

"And the next day you were back on the job again, weren't you?"

"Yes, sir."

"Same place?"

"Yes, sir."

"And you waited during that day until when?"

"Oh, until about four o'clock in the afternoon."

"And then, from your surveillance, you knew that there was no one home, isn't that right?"

"Well, we saw Mrs. Bedford drive off."

"You then *knew* that there was no one home, didn't you?"

"Well, it's hard to *know* anything like that."

"You had been keeping the house under surveillance?"

"We had been, yes."

"For the purpose of finding a time when no one was home?"

"Well, we were just keeping the place under surveillance to see who came and who went."

"And at the first opportunity, when you thought there was no one home, you went and searched the garage?"

"Well . . . I guess that's about right. You can call it that if you want to."

"And you searched the garage but didn't search the house?"

"No, sir, we didn't search the house."

"You searched every inch of the garage, every nook and corner?"

"Yes, sir."

"You waited until you felt certain there was no one home, then you went out to make your search."

"We wanted to make a search of the garage. We didn't want to be interrupted and we didn't want to have anyone interfering with us."

Mason smiled frostily. "You have just said, Mr. Judson, that you wanted to make a search of the garage."

"Well, what's wrong with that? We had a warrant, didn't we?"

"You said of the *garage*."

"I meant of the whole place—the house—the whole business."

"You didn't *say* that. You said you wanted to search the *garage*."

"Well, we had a warrant for it."

166

"Isn't it true," Mason asked, "that the only place you really wanted to search was the garage, and you only wanted to search that because you had been given a tip that the gun would be found in the garage?"

"We were looking for the gun, all right."

"Isn't it a fact that you had a tip before you went out there that the gun would be found in the garage?"

"Objected to as incompetent, irrelevant, and immaterial, not proper cross-examination," Hamilton Burger said.

Judge Strouse thought for a moment. "The objection is overruled . . . if the witness knows."

"I don't know about any tip."

"Isn't it a fact you intended primarily to search the garage?"

"We searched there first."

"Was there some reason you searched there first?"

"That's where we started. We thought we might find a gun there."

"And what made you think that was where the gun was?"

"That was as good a place to hide it as any."

"You mean the police didn't have some anonymous telephone tip to guide you?"

"I mean we searched the garage, looking for a gun, and we found the gun in the garage. I don't know what tip the others had. I was told to go look for a gun."

"In the garage?"

"Well, yes."

"Thank you," Mason said. "That's all."

Arthur Merriam took the stand and testified to experiments he had performed with the gun which he had received from the last witness and which was introduced in evidence. He stated that he had fired test bullets from the gun, had examined them through a comparison microscope, comparing the test bullets with the fatal bullet. He had prepared photographs which showed the identity of striation marks on the two bullets while one was superimposed over the other. These photographs were introduced in evidence.

"You may cross-examine," Hamilton Burger said.

Mason seemed a little bored with the entire proceeding. "No questions," he said.

Hamilton Burger's next witness was a man who had charge of the sporting goods section of one of the large downtown department stores. This man produced records showing the gun in question had been sold to Stewart G. Bedford some five years earlier and that Bedford had signed the register of sales. The book of sales was offered in evidence; then, as a photostatic copy of the original was produced, the Court ordered that the original record might be withdrawn.

"Cross-examine," Hamilton Burger said.

"No questions," Mason announced, suppressing a yawn.

Judge Strouse looked at the clock, said, "It is now time for the afternoon adjournment. The Court admonishes the jurors not to discuss this case among yourselves, nor to permit anyone else to discuss it in your presence. You are not to form or express any opinion until the case is finally submitted to you.

"Court will take a recess until tomorrow morning at ten o'clock."

Bedford gripped Mason's arm. "Mason," he said, "someone planted that gun in my garage."

"Did you put it there?" Mason asked.

"Don't be silly! I tell you I never saw the gun after I went to sleep. That liquor was drugged and someone took the gun out of my brief case, killed Binney Denham, and then subsequently planted the gun in my garage."

"And," Mason pointed out, "telephoned a tip to the police so that the officers would be sure to find it there."

"Well, what does that mean?"

"It means that someone was very anxious that the officers would have plenty of evidence to connect you with the murder."

"And that gets back to this mysterious prowler who was in that motel where Elsa—"

"Just a minute," Mason cautioned. "No names."

"Well, that woman who was in there," Bedford said. "Hang it, Mason! I keep telling you she's important. She's the key to the whole business. Yet you don't seem to get the least bit excited about her, or try to find her."

"How am I going to go about finding her?" Mason asked impatiently. "You tell me there's a needle in a haystack and the needle is important. So what?"

The officer motioned for Bedford to accompany him.

"Hire fifty detectives," Bedford said, holding back momentarily. "Hire a hundred detectives. But *find that woman!*"

"See you tomorrow," Mason told him as the officer led Bedford through the passageway to the jail elevator.

■ 19 ■

PERRY MASON AND DELLA STREET HAD DINNER AT THEIR favorite restaurant, returned for a couple hours' work at the office, and found Elsa Griffin waiting for them in the foyer of the building.

"Hello," Mason said. "Do you want to see me?"

She nodded.

"Been here long?"

"About twenty minutes. I heard you were out to dinner but expected to return to the office this evening, so I waited."

Mason flashed a glance at Della Street. "Something important?"

"I think so."

"Come on up," Mason invited.

The three of them rode up in the elevator and walked down the corridor. Mason opened the door of the private office, went in and switched on the lights.

"Take off your coat and hat," Della Street said. "Sit down in that chair over there."

Elsa Griffin moved quietly, efficiently, as a woman moves who has a fixed purpose and has steeled herself to carry out her objectives in a series of definite steps.

"I had a chance to talk for a few minutes with Mr. Bedford," she said.

Mason nodded.

"A few words of *private* conversation."

"Go ahead," Mason told her.

She said, "Mr. Bedford feels that with all of the resources that he has placed at your command, you could do more about finding that woman who was in my unit there at the motel. Of course, when you come right down to it, *she* could have kept those two units, fifteen and sixteen, under surveillance from my cabin and then gone over and . . . well, at the proper moment she could have simply opened the door of sixteen and fired one shot and then made her escape."

"Yes," Mason said drily, "fired one shot with Bedford's gun."

"Yes," Elsa Griffin said thoughtfully, "I suppose she *would* have had to get into that other cabin and get possession of the gun first. . . . But she *could* have done that, Mr. Mason. She could have gone into the cabin after that blonde went out, and there she found Mr. Bedford asleep. She took the gun from his brief case."

Mason studied her carefully.

Abruptly she said, "Mr. Mason, don't you think it's bad publicity for Mrs. Bedford to wear those horribly heavy dark glasses and keep in the back of the courtroom? Shouldn't she be right up there in front, giving her husband moral support, and not looking as though—as though she were afraid to have people find out who she is?"

"Everyone knows who she is," Mason said. "From the time they started picking the jury, the newspaper people have been interviewing her."

"I know, but she'll never take off those horrid dark glasses. And they make her look terrible. They're great big lensed glasses that completely alter her appearance. She looks just like . . . well, not like herself at all."

"So what would you suggest that I do?" Mason asked.

"Couldn't you tell her to be more natural? Tell her to take her glasses off, to come up and sit as close to her husband as she can to give him a word of encouragement now and then."

"That's what Mr. Bedford wants?"

"I'm satisfied he does. I think that his wife's conduct has hurt him. He acts very differently from the way he normally does. He's . . . well, he's sort of crushed."

"I see," Mason said.

Elsa Griffin was silent for a few minutes, then said, "What have you been able to do with those fingerprints I got for you from the cabin, Mr. Mason?"

"Not very much, I'm afraid. You see, it's very difficult to identify a person unless you have a complete set of ten fingerprints, but as one who studied to be a detective, you know all about that."

"Yes, I suppose so," she said dubiously. "I thought Mr. Brems gave a very good description of that prowler who was in my cabin."

Mason nodded.

"There's something about the way he describes her, something about her walk. I almost feel that I know her. It's the most peculiar feeling. It's like seeing a face that you can't place, yet which is very familiar to you.

You know it as well as you know your own, and yet somehow you can't get it fixed with the name. You just can't get the right connection. There's one link in the chain that's missing."

Again Mason nodded.

"I have a feeling that if I could only think of that, I'd have it. I feel that there's a solution to the whole business just almost at our finger tips, and yet it keeps eluding us like . . . like a Halloween apple."

Mason sat silent.

"Well," she said, getting to her feet, "I must be going. I wanted to tell you Mr. Bedford would like very much indeed to have you concentrate all of the resources at your command on finding that woman. Also, I'm satisfied he would like it a lot better if his wife wouldn't act as though she were afraid of being recognized. You know, really, she's a very beautiful woman and she has a wonderful carriage—"

Abruptly Elsa Griffin ceased speaking and looked at Mason with eyes that slowly widened with startled, incredulous surprise.

"What's the matter?" Mason asked. "What is it?"

"My God!" she exclaimed. "It *couldn't* be!"

"Come on," Mason said. "What is it?"

"Are you ill?" Della Street asked.

She kept looking at him with round, startled eyes.

"Good heavens, Mr. Mason! It's just hit me like a ton of bricks. Let me sit down."

She dropped down into a chair, moved her head slowly from side to side, looking around the office as though some mental shock had left her completely disoriented.

"Well," Mason asked, "what is it?"

"I was just mentioning Mrs. Bedford and thinking about her carriage and the way she walks and . . . Mr. Mason, it's just come to me. It's a terrible thing. It's just as though something had crashed into my mind."

"What is it?" Mason asked.

"Don't you see, Mr. Mason? That prowler who was in my unit at the motel. The description Mr. Brems gave fits her perfectly. Why, you couldn't ask for a better description of Mrs. Bedford than the one that Morrison Brems gave."

Mason sat silent, his eyes steadily studying Elsa Griffin's face. Abruptly she snapped her fingers.

"I have it, Mr. Mason! I have it! You've got her photograph on that police card—her photograph and her fingerprints. You could compare the latents I took there in my unit in the motel with her fingerprints on there, and . . . and then we'd *know!*"

Mason nodded to Della Street. "Get the card with Mrs. Bedford's fingerprints, Della. Also, get the envelope with the unidentified latent prints. You'll remember we discarded Elsa Griffin's prints. We have four unidentified latents numbered fourteen, sixteen, nine, and twelve. I'd like to have those prints, please."

Della Street regarded Mason's expressionless face for a moment, then went to the locked filing case in which the lawyer kept matters to which he was referring in cases under trial, and returned with the articles Mason had requested.

Elsa Griffin eagerly reached for the envelope with the lifted fingerprints, took the cards from the envelope, examined them carefully, then grabbed the card containing Ann Roann Bedford's criminal record.

She swiftly compared the lifted latent prints with those on the card, looking intently from one to the other. Gradually her excitement became evident, then mounted to a fever pitch.

"Mr. Mason, these prints are hers!"

Mason took the card with Mrs. Bedford's criminal record. Elsa Griffin held onto the cards numbered fourteen, sixteen, nine, and twelve.

"They're hers, Mr. Mason! You can take my word for it. I've studied fingerpinting."

Mason said, "Let's hope you're mistaken. That would *really* put the fat in the fire. We simply couldn't have that."

Elsa Griffin picked up the envelope containing the lifted latents. "Mr. Mason," she said sternly, "you're representing Stewart G. Bedford. You *have* to represent his interests regardless of who gets hurt."

Mason held out his hand for the latent prints. She drew back slightly. "You can't be a traitor to his cause in order to protect . . . to protect the person who got him into all this trouble in the first place."

Mason said, "A lawyer has to protect his client's *best* interests. That doesn't mean he necessarily has to do what the client wants or what the client's friends may want. He must do what is best for the client."

"You mean you aren't going to tell Mr. Bedford that it was his own wife who, goaded to desperation by this blackmailer, finally decided to—"

"No," Mason interrupted, "I'm not going to tell him, and I don't want you to tell him."

She suddenly jumped from her chair, and raced for the exit door of the office.

"Come back here," Della Street cried, making a grab and missing Elsa Griffin's flying skirt by a matter of inches.

Before Della Street could get to the door, Elsa Griffin had wrenched it open.

Sergeant Holcomb was standing on the outer threshold. "Well, well, good evening, folks," he said, slipping an arm around Elsa Griffin's shoulders. "I gather there has been a little commotion in here. What's going on?"

"This young woman is trying to take some personal property which doesn't belong to her," Mason said.

"Well, well, well, isn't that interesting? Stealing from you, eh? Could you describe the property, Mason? Perhaps you'd like to go down to headquarters and swear out a complaint, charging her with larceny. What's your side of the story, Miss Griffin?"

Elsa Griffin pushed the lifted latents inside the front of her dress. "Will you," she asked Sergeant Holcomb, "kindly escort me home and then see that I am subpoenaed as a witness for the prosecution? I think it's time someone showed Mr. Perry Mason, the great criminal lawyer, that it's against the law to condone murder and conceal evidence from the police."

Sergeant Holcomb's face was wreathed in smiles. "Sister," he said, "you've made a *great* little speech. You just come along with me."

■ 20 ■

Hamilton Burger, his face plainly indicating his feelings, rose to his feet when court was called to order the next morning and said, "Your Honor, I would like to call the Court's attention to Section 135 of the penal code, which reads as follows: 'Every person who, knowing that any book, paper, record, instrument in writing, or other matter or thing, is about to be produced in evidence upon any trial, inquiry, or investigation whatever, authorized by law, willfully destroys *or conceals* the same, with intent thereby to prevent it from being produced is guilty of a misdemeanor.'"

Judge Strouse, plainly puzzled, said, "The Court is, I think, familiar with the law, Mr. Burger."

"Yes, Your Honor," Hamilton Burger said. "I merely wished to call the section to Your Honor's attention. I know Your Honor is familiar with the law. I feel that perhaps some other persons are not, and now, Your Honor, I wish to call Miss Elsa Griffin to the stand."

Stewart Bedford looked at Mason with alarm. "What the devil's this?" he whispered. "I thought we were going to keep her out of the public view. We can't afford to have Brems recognize her as the one who was in unit twelve."

"She didn't like the way I was handling things," Mason said. "She decided to become a witness."

"When did that happen?"

"Late last night."

"You didn't tell me."

"I didn't want to worry you."

The outer door opened, and Elsa Griffin, her chin high, came marching into the courtroom. She raised her right hand, was sworn, and took the witness stand.

"What is your name?" Hamilton Burger asked.

"Elsa Griffin."

"Are you acquainted with the defendant in this case?"

"I am employed by him."

"Where were you on the sixth day of April of this year?"

"I was at The Staylonger Motel."

"What were you doing there?"

"I was there at the request of a certain person."

"Now then, if the Court please," Hamilton Burger said, addressing Judge Strouse, "a most unusual situation is about to develop. I may state that this witness, while wishing the authorities to take certain action, did nevertheless conspire with another person, whom I shall presently name, to conceal and suppress certain evidence which we consider highly pertinent.

"I had this witness placed under subpoena. She is here as an unwilling witness. That is, she is not only willing but anxious to testify to certain phases of the case. However, she is quite unwilling to testify as to other matters. As to these matters she has refused to make any

176

statement, and I have no knowledge of how much or how little she knows as to this part of the case. She simply will not talk with me except upon one point.

"It is, therefore, necessary for me to approach this witness upon certain matters as a hostile witness."

"Perhaps," Judge Strouse said, "you had better first examine the witness upon the matters as to which she is willing to give her testimony, and then elicit information from her on the other points as a hostile witness, and under the rules pertaining to the examination of hostile witnesses."

"Very well, Your Honor."

Hamilton Burger turned to the witness.

"You are now and for several years have been employed by the defendant?"

"Yes."

"In what capacity?"

"I am his confidential secretary."

"Are you acquainted with Mr. Morrison Brems, the manager of The Staylonger Motel?"

"Yes."

"Did you have a conversation with Morrison Brems on April sixth of this year?"

"Yes."

"When?"

"Early in the evening."

"What was said at that conversation?"

"Objected to as incompetent, irrelevant, and immaterial," Mason said.

"Just a moment, Your Honor," Hamilton Burger countered. "We propose to show that this witness was at the time of this conversation the agent of the defendant, that she went to the motel in accordance with instructions issued by the defendant."

"You had better show that first then," Judge Strouse ruled.

"But that, Your Honor, is where we are having trouble, that is one of the points where the witness is hostile."

"There are some other matters on which the witness is not a hostile witness?" Judge Strouse asked.

"Yes."

"The Court has suggested that you proceed with those matters until the evidence which can be produced by this witness as a friendly witness is all before the Court. Then, if there are other matters on which the witness is hostile, and you request permission to deal with the witness as a hostile witness, the record will be straight as to what has been done and where, when and why it has been done."

"Very well, Your Honor."

Hamilton Burger turned again to the witness. "After this conversation did you return to The Staylonger Motel later on in the evening of April sixth?"

"Actually it was, I believe, early on the morning of April seventh."

"Who sent you to The Staylonger Motel?"

"Mr. Perry Mason."

"You mean that you received instructions from Mr. Mason while he was acting as attorney for Stewart G. Bedford, the defendant in this case?"

"Yes."

"What did Mr. Mason instruct you to do?"

"To get certain fingerprints from unit twelve, to take a fingerprint outfit and dust every place in the unit where I thought I could get a suitable latent fingerprint, to lift those fingerprints and then to obliterate every single remaining fingerprint which might be in unit twelve, after that to bring the lifted fingerprints to Mr. Mason."

"Did you understand the process of taking fingerprints and lifting them?"

"Yes."

"Had you made some study of that process?"

"Yes."

"Where?"

"I am a graduate of a correspondence school dealing with such matters."

"Where did you get the material necessary to lift latent fingerprints?"

"Mr. Mason furnished it."

"And what did you do after Mr. Mason gave you those materials?"

"I went to the motel and lifted certain fingerprints from unit twelve as I had been instructed."

"And then what?"

"I took those fingerprints to Mr. Mason so that the fingerprints which were mine could be discarded, and thereby, through a process of elimination, leave only the fingerprints of any person who had been prowling the cabin during my absence."

"Do you know if this was done?"

"It was done. I was so advised by Mr. Mason, who also told me that all the latent prints I had lifted were my prints, with the exception of those prints contained on four cards."

"Do you know what four cards these were?"

"Yes. As I lifted prints I put them on cards and numbered the cards. The cards containing the significant prints were numbered fourteen, sixteen, nine, and twelve.

"Fourteen and sixteen came from the glass doorknob of the closet door in the motel unit; nine and twelve came from the side of a mirror."

"Do you know where these four cards are now?"

"Yes."

"Where?"

"I have them."

"Where did you get them?"

"I snatched them from Perry Mason last night and ran to the police as Mr. Mason was trying to get them back."

"Did you give them to the police?"

"No."

"Why?"

"I didn't want anything to happen to them. You see by last night I knew whose prints they were. That is why I ran with them."

"Why did you feel that you had to run?" Burger asked.

Judge Strouse glanced down at Perry Mason expectantly. When the lawyer made no effort to object, Judge Strouse said to the witness, "Just a minute before you answer that question. Does the defense wish to object to this question, Mr. Mason?"

"No, Your Honor," Perry Mason said. "I feel that I am being on trial here and that therefore I should let the full facts come out."

Judge Strouse frowned. "You may feel that you are on trial, Mr. Mason. That is a matter of dispute. There can be no dispute that your client is on trial, and your primary duty is to protect the interests of that client regardless of the effect on your own private affairs."

"I understand that, Your Honor."

"This question seems to me to be argumentative and calls for a conclusion of the witness."

"There is no objection, Your Honor."

Judge Strouse hesitated and said, "I would like to point out to you, Mr. Mason, that the Court will take a hand if it appears that your interests in the case become adverse to your client and no objection is made to questions which are detrimental to your client's case."

"I think if the Court please," Mason said, "the opposite may be the case here. I feel that the answer of the witness may be strongly opposed to my personal interests but very much in favor of the defendant's case. You see that is the reason the witness is both a willing witness on some phases of the case and an unwilling witness on others. She feels that she should testify against me, but she is loyal to the interests of her employer."

"Very well," Judge Strouse said. "If you don't wish to object, the witness will answer the question."

"Answer the question," Hamilton Burger said. "Why did you feel that you had to run?"

"Because at that time I had identified those fingerprints."

"You had?"

"Yes, sir."

"You said that you had studied fingerprinting?"

"Yes."

"And you were able at that time to identify these fingerprints?"

"Yes, sir."

"You compared them with originals?"

"Well, enough to know whose they were."

Hamilton Burger turned to the Court and said, "I confess, Your Honor, that on some of these matters I am feeling my way because of the peculiar situation which exists. The witness promised to give her testimony on the stand but would not tell me—"

"There is no objection," Judge Strouse interrupted. "There is, therefore, nothing before the Court. You will kindly refrain from making any argument or comments as to the testimony of this witness until it comes time to argue the matter to the jury. Simply proceed with your question and answer, Mr. District Attorney."

"Yes, Your Honor," Hamilton Burger said.

Judge Strouse looked down at Mason. His expression was thoughtfully dubious.

"You yourself were able to identify those prints?" Hamilton Burger asked.

"Yes, sir."

"Whose prints did you think they were?"

"Now just a minute," Judge Strouse said. "Apparently counsel is not going to object that no proper foundation has been laid and that this calls for an opinion of the witness. Miss Griffin?"

"Yes, Your Honor?"

"You state that you studied fingerprinting?"

"Yes, I did, Your Honor."

"How?"

"By correspondence."

"Over what period of time?"

"I took a complete course. I graduated. I learned to distinguish the different characteristics of fingerprints. I learned how to take fingerprints and compare them and how to classify them."

"Is there any objection from defense counsel?" Judge Strouse asked.

"None whatever," Mason said.

"Very well, whose prints were they?" Burger asked.

"Now just a minute," Mason said. "If the Court please I feel that that question is improper."

"I feel the objection is in order," Judge Strouse ruled.

"However," Mason went on, "I am not interposing the objection which perhaps Your Honor has in mind. I feel that this witness, while she may have qualified as an expert on fingerpinting, has qualified as a limited expert. She is what might be called an amateur expert. I feel that, therefore, the question should not be as to whose fingerprints these were, but in her opinion, for what it may be worth, what points of similarity there are between these prints and known standards."

Judge Strouse said, "The objection is sustained."

Hamilton Burger, his face darkening with annoyance, asked, "In your opinion, for what it may be worth, what points of similarity are there between these latents and the known prints of any person with which you may have made a comparison?"

Elsa Griffin raised her head. Her defiant eyes glared at the defendant, then at Mason, and then turned to the jury. In a firm voice she said, "In my opinion, for what it may be worth, these prints have so many points of similarity I can say they were made by the fingers of Mrs. Stewart G. Bedford, the wife of the defendant in this case."

Hamilton Burger grinned. "Do you have those fingerprints with you?"

"I do."

"And how do you identify them?"

"The cards are numbered," she said. "The numbers are fourteen, sixteen, nine, and twelve respectively. Also I signed my name on the backs of these cards at a late hour last night so that there could be no possibility of substitution or mistake. I did that at the suggestion of the district attorney. He wanted me to leave these cards with him. When I refused he asked me to sign my name so there could be no possibility of trickery."

Hamilton Burger was grinning. "And then what did I do, if anything?"

"Then you signed your name beneath mine and put the date on the cards."

"I ask of the Court please that those prints be introduced in evidence," Hamilton Burger said, "as People's Exhibit under proper numbers."

"Now just a moment," Mason said. "At this point, Your Honor, I feel that I have a right to a *voir dire* examination as to the authenticity of the exhibits."

"Go ahead," Hamilton Burger said. "In fact, handle your cross-examination on this phase of the case if you want, because from here on the witness becomes an unwilling witness."

"Counsel may proceed," Judge Strouse said.

"You made this positive identification of the latent prints last night, Miss Griffin?"

"Yes."

"In my office?"

"Yes."

"You were rather excited at the time?"

"Well . . . all right, I *was* a little excited, but I wasn't too excited to compare fingerprints."

"You checked all four of these fingerprints?"

"Yes."

"All four of them were the fingerprints of Mrs. Bedford?"

"Yes."

Bedford tugged at Mason's coat. "Look here, Mason," he whispered. "Don't let her—"

Mason brushed his client's hand to one side. "Keep quiet," he ordered."

Mason arose and approached the witness stand. "You are, I believe, skilled in classifying fingerprints?"

"I am."

"You know how to do it?"

"Very well."

Mason said, "I am going to give you a magnifying glass to assist you in looking at these prints."

Mason took a powerful pocket magnifying glass from his pocket, turned to the clerk, and said, "May I have some of the fingerprints which have been introduced in evidence? I don't care for the fingerprints of the defendant which were found in the car and in the motel, but I would like some of those other exhibits of the unidentified party, the ones that were found in the car and in the motel."

"Very well," the clerk said, thumbing through the exhibits. He handed Mason several of the cards.

"Now then," Mason said, "I call your attention to People's Exhibit number twenty-eight, which purports to be a lifted fingerprint. I will ask you to look at that and see if that fingerprint matches one on any of the cards numbered fourteen, sixteen, nine, and twelve, which you have produced."

The witness made a show of studying the print with the magnifying glass, shook her head and said, "No!" and then added, "It can't. These prints are the prints of Mrs. Bedford. Those prints in the exhibits are the prints of an unidentified person."

"But isn't it true that this unidentified person, as far

as you know, might well have been Mrs. Bedford?" Mason asked.

"No, that person was a blonde. I saw her."

"But you don't know that it was the blonde who left the prints?"

"No, I don't *know* that."

"Then please examine this print closely."

Mason held the print out to Elsa Griffin, who looked at it with the magnifying glass in a perfunctory manner, then handed it back to Mason.

"Now," Mason said, "I call your attention to People's Exhibit number thirty-four, and ask you to compare this."

Again the witness made a perfunctory study with the magnifying glass and said, "No. None of these prints match."

"None of them?" Mason asked.

"None! I tell you, Mr. Mason, those are the prints of Mrs. Bedford, and you know it as well as I do."

Mason appeared to be somewhat rebuffed. He studied the prints, then looked at the cards in Elsa Griffin's hand.

"Perhaps," he said, "you can tell me just how you go about examining a fingerprint. Take this one, for instance, on the card numbered sixteen. That is one, I believe, that you secured from the under side of a glass doorknob in the cabin?"

"Yes."

"Now what is the first characteristic of that print which you noticed?"

"That is a tented arch."

"I see. A tented arch," Mason said thoughtfully. "Now would you mind pointing out just where that tented arch is? Oh, I see. Now this fingerprint which I hand you which has been numbered People's Exhibit number thirty-seven also has a tented arch, does it not?"

She looked at the print and said, "Yes."

"Now, using this print number sixteen which you say

you recovered from the closet doorknob, let us count from the tented arch through the ridges until we come to a branch in the ridges. There are, let's see, one, two, three, four, five, six, seven, eight ridges, and then we come to a branch."

"That is right," she said.

"Well, now let's see," Mason said. "We take this print which has been introduced by the prosecution as number thirty-seven and we count—let's see, why, yes, we count the same number of ridges and we come to the same peculiar branching, do we not?"

"Let me see," the witness said.

She studied the print through the magnifying glass. "Well, yes," she said, "that is what you would call *one* point of similarity. You need several to make a perfect identification."

"I see," Mason said. "One point of similarity could of course be a coincidence."

"Don't make any mistake, Mr. Mason," she said icily. "That *is* a coincidence."

"Very well, now, let's look at your print number sixteen again, the one which you got from underneath the closet doorknob, and see if you can find some other distinguishing mark."

"You have one here," she said. "On the tenth ridge."

"The tenth," Mason said. "Let me see . . . oh, yes."

"Well, now let's look at thirty-seven again, and see if you can find the same point of similarity there."

"There's no use looking," she said. "There won't be."

"Tut, tut!" Mason said. "Don't jump at conclusions, Miss Griffin. You're testifying as an expert, so let's just take a look now if you please. Count up these ridges and—"

The witness gasped.

"Do you find such a point of similarity?" Mason asked, seemingly as much surprised as the witness.

"I . . . I seem to. Somebody has been tampering with these fingerprints."

"Now, just a moment! Just a moment!" Hamilton Burger said. "This is a serious matter, Your Honor."

"Who's going to tamper with the fingerprints?" Mason asked. "The fingerprints that the witness has been testifying to were in her possession. She said that she had them in her possession all night. She wouldn't let them out of her possession for fear they might be tampered with. She signed her name on the back of each card. The district attorney signed his name and wrote the date. There are the signatures on the cards. These other cards are exhibits which the prosecution introduced in court. I have just taken those exhibits from the clerk. They bear the file number of the clerk and the exhibit number."

"Just the same," Hamilton Burger shouted, "there's some sort of a flimflam here. The witness knows it and I know it."

"Mr. Burger," Judge Strouse stated, "you will not make any such charges in this courtroom. Not unless they can be substantiated. Apparently there is no possibility of any substitution. Miss Griffin?"

"Yes, Your Honor?"

"Kindly look at the card numbered sixteen."

"Yes, Your Honor."

"You got that card last night?"

"I . . . I . . . yes, I must have."

"From the office of Perry Mason?"

"Yes."

"And you compared that card *at that time* with the fingerprints of Mrs. Stewart Bedford?"

"Yes, Your Honor."

"That card was in your possession and under your control at that time?"

"Yes, Your Honor."

"Now, speaking for the moment as to this one card,

exactly what did you do with that card *after* satisfying yourself the print was that of Mrs. Bedford? What did you do with it?"

"I put it in the front of my dress."

"And then what?"

"I was escorted by Sergeant Holcomb to the office of Hamilton Burger. Mr. Burger wanted to have me leave the prints with him. I refused to do so. At his suggestion, I signed my name on the back of each card. Then he signed his name and the date, so there could be no question of a substitution, so that I couldn't substitute them, and so that no one else could."

"And that's your signature and the date on the back of that card?"

"It seems to be but . . . I'm not certain. May I examine these prints for a moment?"

"Take all the time you want," Judge Strouse said.

Hamilton Burger said, "Your Honor, I feel that there should be some inquiry here. This is completely in accordance with the peculiar phenomena which always seem to occur in cases where Mr. Perry Mason is defense counsel."

"I resent that," Perry Mason said. "I am simply trying to cross-examine this expert, this so-called expert, I may add."

Elsa Griffin looked up from the fingerprint classification to flash him a glance of venomous hatred.

Judge Strouse said, "Counsel for both sides will return to their chairs at counsel tables. The witness will be given ample opportunity to make the comparison which she wishes."

Burger reluctantly lumbered back to his chair at the prosecution's table and dropped into it.

Mason walked back, sat down, locked his hands behind his head and, with elaborate unconcern, leaned back in the chair.

Stewart Bedford tried to whisper to him, but Mason waved him back into silence.

The witness proceeded to examine the cards, studying first one and then the other, counting ridges with a sharp-pointed pencil. The silence in the courtroom grew to a peak of tension.

Suddenly Elsa Griffin threw the magnifying glass directly at Perry Mason. The glass hit the mahogany table, bounced against the lawyer's chest. Elsa Griffin dropped all the fingerprint cards, put her hands to her eyes, and began to cry hysterically.

Mason got to his feet.

Judge Strouse said, "Just a moment. Counsel for both sides will remain seated. The Court wants to examine the witness. Miss Griffin, will you kindly regain your composure. The Court wishes to ask you certain questions."

She took her hands from her face, raised tearful eyes to the Court. "What is it?" she asked.

"Do you now conclude that your print number sixteen is the same as the print which has been introduced in evidence, prosecution's number thirty-seven—that both were made by the same finger?"

She said, "It is, Your Honor, but it *wasn't*. Last night it *was* the print of Mrs. Bedford. Somebody somewhere has mixed everything all up, and . . . and now I don't know what I'm doing, or what I'm talking about."

"Well, there's no reason to be hysterical about this, Miss Griffin," Judge Strouse said. "You're certain that this fingerprint number sixteen is the one that you took from the cottage?"

She nodded. "It has to be . . . I . . . I *know* that it's Mrs. Bedford's fingerprint!"

"There certainly can be no doubt about the authenticity of the Court Exhibit," Judge Strouse said. "Now apparently, according to the testimony of the prosecution's witness, the identity of these fingerprints simply means that the same woman who was in unit sixteen of the motel on April sixth was also in unit twelve of the motel on that same day, that this person also drove the rented automobile."

Elsa Griffin shook her head. "It isn't so, Your Honor. It simply can't be. It isn't—" Again she lapsed into a storm of tears.

Hamilton Burger said, "If the Court please, may I make a suggestion?"

"What is it?" Judge Strouse asked coldly.

Hamilton Burger said, "This witness seems to be emotionally upset. I suggest that she be withdrawn from the stand. I suggest that the four cards, each bearing her signature and the numbers fourteen, sixteen, nine, and twelve, be each stamped by the clerk for identification; that these cards then be given to the police fingerprint expert who is here in the witness room and who can very shortly give us an opinion as to the identity of those fingerprints. In the meantime, I wish to state to the Court that I am completely satisfied with the sincerity and integrity of this witness. I personally feel that there has been some trickery and substitution. I think that a deception and a fraud is being practiced on this court and in order to prove it I would ask to recall Morrison Brems, the manager of the motel, to the stand."

Judge Strouse stroked his chin. "The jury will disregard the comments of the district attorney," he said, "in regard to deception or fraud. This witness will be excused from the stand, the cards will be marked for identification by the clerk and then delivered to the fingerprint expert who has previously testified and who will be charged by the court with making a comparison and a report. Now in the meantime the witness Brems will come forward. You will be excused for the time being, Miss Griffin. Just leave the stand, if you will, and try to compose yourself."

The bailiff escorted the sobbing Elsa Griffin from the stand.

Morrison Brems was brought into court.

"I am now going to prove my point another way," Hamilton Burger said. "Mr. Brems, you have already been sworn in this case. You talked with this so-called prowler who emerged from unit number twelve?"

"Yes, sir."

"You saw that prowler leaving the cabin?"

"Yes, sir."

Hamilton Burger said, "I am going to ask Mrs. Stewart G. Bedford, who is in court, to stand up and take off the heavy dark glasses with which she has effectively kept her identity concealed. I am going to ask her to walk across the courtroom in front of this witness."

"Object," Bedford whispered frantically to Mason. "Object. Stop this! Don't let him get away with it!"

"Keep quiet," Mason warned. "If we object now we'll antagonize the jury. Let him go."

"Stand up, Mrs. Bedford," Judge Strouse ordered.

Mrs. Bedford got to her feet.

"Will you kindly remove your glasses?"

"This isn't the proper way of making an identification," Perry Mason said. "There should be a line-up, Your Honor, but we have no objection."

"Come inside the rail here, Mrs. Bedford, right through that gate," Judge Strouse directed. "Now just walk the length of the courtroom, if you will, turn your face to the witness, and—"

"That's the one. That's the one. That's the woman!" Morrison Brems shouted, excitedly.

Ann Roann Bedford stopped abruptly in her stride. She turned to face the witness. "You lie," she said, her voice cold with venom.

Judge Strouse banged his gavel. "There will be no comments except in response to questions asked by counsel," he said. "You may return to your seat, Mrs. Bedford, and you will please refrain from making any comment. Proceed, Mr. Burger."

A grinning Hamilton Burger turned to Perry Mason and made an exaggerated bow. "And now, Mr. Mason," he said, "you may cross-examine—to your heart's content."

"Now just a moment, Mr. District Attorney," Judge Strouse snapped. "That last comment was uncalled for; that is not proper conduct."

"I beg the Court's pardon," Hamilton Burger said, his face suffused with triumph. "I think, if the Court please, I can soon suggest to the Court what happened to the fingerprint evidence, but I'll be *very* glad to hear Mr. Mason cross-examine *this* witness and see what can be done with *his* testimony. However, I do beg the Court's pardon."

"Proceed with the cross-examination," Judge Strouse said to Perry Mason.

Perry Mason rose to his full height, faced Morrison Brems on the stand.

"Have you ever been convicted of a felony, Mr. Brems?"

The witness recoiled as though Mason had struck him.

Hamilton Burger, on his feet, was shouting, "Your Honor, Your Honor! Counsel can't *do* that! That's misconduct! Unless he has some grounds to believe—"

"You can always impeach a witness by showing he has been convicted of a felony," Mason said as Hamilton Burger hesitated, sputtering in his rage.

"Of course you can, of course you can," Hamilton Burger yelled. "But you can't ask questions like that where you haven't anything on which to base such a charge. That's misconduct! That's—"

"Suppose you let him answer the question," Mason said, "and then—"

"It's misconduct! That's unprofessional. That's—"

"I think," Judge Strouse said, "the objection will be overruled. The witness will answer the question."

"Remember," Mason warned, "you're under oath. I'm

asking you the direct question. Have you ever been convicted of a felony?"

The witness who had been so sure of himself as he had regarded Mason a few short seconds earlier seemed to shrivel inside his clothes. He shifted his position uncomfortably. The courtroom silence became oppressive.

"Have you?" Mason asked.

"Yes," Brems said.

"How many times?"

"Three."

"Did you ever use the alias of Harry Elston?"

The witness again hesitated. "You're under oath," Mason reminded him, "and a handwriting expert is going to check your handwriting, so be careful what you say."

"I refuse to answer," the witness said with a sudden desperate attempt at collecting himself. "I refuse to answer on the ground that to do so may incriminate me."

"And," Mason went on, "on the seventh day of April of this year you called on your accomplice Grace Compton who had occupied unit sixteen at The Staylonger Motel on April sixth under the name of Mrs. S. G. Wilfred, and beat her up because she had been talking with me, didn't you?

"Now just a minute, Mr. Brems. Before you answer that question, remember that I had a private detective shadowing Miss Compton, shadowing the apartment house where she lived, noticing the people who went in and out of the apartment, and that I am at the present time in touch with Grace Compton in Acapulco. Now answer the question, did you or didn't you?"

"I refuse to answer," the witness said, "on the ground that to do so might incriminate ne."

Mason turned to the judge, conscious of the open-mouthed jurors literally sitting on the edges of their chairs.

"And now, Your Honor, I suggest that the Court take a recess until we can have an opinion of the police fingerprint expert on these fingerprints and so the police will have some opportunity to reinvestigate the murder."

Mason sat down.

"In view of the situation," Judge Strouse said, "Court will take a recess until two o'clock this afternoon."

■ 21 ■

STEWART BEDFORD, DELLA STREET, PAUL DRAKE, AND Mason sat in Mason's office.

Bedford rubbed his hands over his eyes. "Those damn newspaper photographers," he said. "They've exploded so many flashbulbs in my face I'm completely blinded."

"You'll get over it in an hour or so," Mason told him. "But you'd better let Paul Drake drive you home."

"He won't need to," Bedford said. "My wife is on her way up here. Tell me, Mason, how the devil did *you* know what had happened?"

"I had a few leads to work on," Mason said. "Your story about the hit-and-run accident was of course something you thought up. Therefore, the blackmailers couldn't have anticipated that. But the blackmailers *did* know that you were at The Staylonger Motel because of blackmail which had been levied because of your wife. In order to get a perfect case against you, they wanted to bring your wife into it. Therefore, Morrison Brems, apparently as the thoroughly respectable manager of the motel, stated that he had seen a prowler emerging from unit twelve.

"When you and Grace Compton went out for lunch, Brems realized this was the logical time to drug the whisky, then kill Denham with your gun, loot the lock box which had been held in joint tenancy, and blame the crime on you with the motivation being your desire to stop a continuing blackmail of you and your wife.

"For that reason, Brems wanted to direct suspicion to your wife. Elsa Griffin hadn't fooled him any when she registered under an assumed name and juggled the figures of her license number. So Brems invented this mysterious prowler whom he said he had seen coming out of unit twelve. He gave an absolutely perfect and very detailed description of your wife, one that was so complete that almost anyone who knew her should have recognized her."

"But, look here, Mason, *I* picked that motel."

Mason grinned. "You thought you did. When you check back on the circumstances, you'll realize that at a certain point the blonde told you the coast was clear and to pick any motel. The first one you passed after that was a shabby, second-rate motel. You didn't want that and the blackmailers knew you wouldn't.

"The next one was The Staylonger and you picked that. If you hadn't, the blonde would have steered you in there anyway. You picked it the same way the man from the audience picks out a card from the deck handed him by the stage magician."

"But what about those fingerprints? How did Elsa Griffin get so badly fooled?"

"Elsa," Mason said, "was the first one to swallow the story of Morrison Brems. She fell for it, hook, line, and sinker. As soon as she heard the description of that woman, she became absolutely convinced that your wife had been down there at the motel. She felt certain that, if that had been the case, your wife must have been the one who killed Binney Denham. She wasn't going to say anything unless it appeared your safety was jeopardized.

"I sent her back down to unit twelve in order to get latent fingerprints. She was down there for hours. She had plenty of time not only to get the latent fingerprints, but to compare them as she took them. That is, she compared them with her own prints and when she did she found, to her chagrin, that she hadn't been able to lift a single fingerprint which hadn't been made by her. Yet she was absolutely certain in her own mind that your wife had been down there at the cabin. What she did was thoroughly logical under the circumstances. She was completely loyal to you. She had no loyalty and little affection for your wife. In spite of your instructions she had preserved those fingerprints which had been lifted from the back of the cocktail tray, so after she left the motel she drove to her apartment, got those prints, put numbers on the cards that fitted them in with the prints she was surrendering, and turned the whole batch in to me.

"She knew absolutely then that by the time her fingerprints had been eliminated there would be four prints of your wife left. She didn't intend to do anything about it unless the situation got desperate. Then she intended to use those prints to save you from being convicted.

"I will admit that there was a period when I myself was pretty much concerned about it. Elsa, of course, thought that your wife had worn gloves while she was in the cabin and so hadn't left any fingerprints. I thought that your wife was the one who had been in the cabin until I became fully convinced that she hadn't been."

"Then what did you do?"

"Then," Mason said, "it was very simple. I had fingerprints lifted from Grace Compton's apartment. I placed four of the best of those in my safe. I put the same numbers on the cards that Elsa had put on her cards."

Paul Drake shook his head. "You pulled a fast one there, Perry. They can sure get you for that."

"Get me for what?" Mason asked.

"Substituting evidence."

"I didn't substitute any evidence."

"There's a law on that," Drake said.

"Sure there is," Mason said, "but I didn't substitute any evidence. I told Della Street to get me fourteen, sixteen, twelve, and nine from the safe. That's what she did. Of course, I can't help it if there were two sets of cards with numbers on them, and if Della got the wrong set. That wasn't a substitution. Of course, if Elsa Griffin had asked me if those were the prints she had given me, then I would have had to acknowledge that they weren't, or else have been guilty of deceiving the witness and concealing evidence, but she didn't ask me that question. Neither did she really compare the prints. Since she *knew* these prints she had given me belonged to Mrs. Bedford she simply pretended to make a comparison, then she grabbed the prints and made for the door, where she had arranged to have Sergeant Holcomb waiting. Under the circumstances, I wasn't required to volunteer any information."

"But how the devil did you *know?*" Bedford asked.

Mason said, "It was quite simple. I knew that your wife hadn't left any fingerprints in the cabin because I knew she hadn't been there. Since the description given by Morrison Brems was so completely realistic down to the last detail and fitted your wife so exactly, I knew that Morrison Brems was lying. We all knew that Binney Denham had some hidden accomplice in the background. That is, we felt he did. After Grace Compton had been beaten up because she had talked with me, I knew there must be another accomplice. Who then could that accomplice be?

"The most logical person was Morrison Brems. Binney Denham wanted to pull his blackmailing stunts at a friendly motel where he was in partnership with the manager. You'll probably find that this motel was one of their big sources of income. Morrison Brems ran that motel. When people whose manner looked a little bit surreptitious registered there, Morrison Brems made it a point to check their baggage and their registration and find out who they were. Then the information was relayed to Binney Denham and that's where a lot of Denham's blackmail material came from.

"They made the mistake of trying to gild the lily. They were so anxious to see that your wife was brought into it that they described her as having been down there. The police hadn't connected up the description, but Brems certainly intended to see that they did before the case was over. Elsa Griffin connected it up as soon as she heard it, and kept pestering you to get after me to find the woman who had been down there. When I didn't move fast enough to suit her, she decided to bring in the fingerprints.

"Because she knew they were fingerprints that had been taken from the silver platter and not from the motel where she said she found them, she only went through the motions of comparing them. She was so certain whose prints they were that she just didn't bother to look for distinguishing characcertistics."

"But," Bedford asked, "how did you know they were gilding the lily, Mason? How did you know my wife hadn't been down there?"

Mason looked him in the eyes. "I asked her if she had been there," he said, "and she assured me she hadn't."

"And you did this whole thing, you staked your reputation and everything on her word?"

Mason, still looking at Bedford, said, "In this business, Bedford, you get to be a pretty damn good judge of character or else you don't last long."

"I still don't see how you knew that Brems had a criminal record."

Mason grinned. "I was simply relying on the law of averages and of character. It would have been as impossible for Morrison Brems to have lived as long as he has with the type of mind he has without having a criminal record as it would have been for your wife to have looked me in the eyes and lied about having gone to that cabin."

Knuckles tapped gently on the door of Mason's office.

"That'll be Ann Roann now," Bedford said, getting to his feet. "Mason, how the devil can I ever thank you enough for what you have done?"

Mason's answer was laconic. "Just write thanks underneath your signature when you make out the check."